ART LESSONS

ART LESSONS

A NOVEL

KATHERINE KOLLER

For Sterling, from one artist to another.
Katharine Koller 🌲

ENFIELD
&WIZENTY

Enfield & Wizenty
(an imprint of Great Plains Publications)
233 Garfield Street
Winnipeg, MB R3G 2M1
www.greatplains.mb.ca

Great Plains Publications gratefully acknowledges the financial support provided for its publishing program by the Government of Canada through the Canada Book Fund; the Canada Council for the Arts; the Province of Manitoba through the Book Publishing Tax Credit and the Book Publisher Marketing Assistance Program; and the Manitoba Arts Council.

Design & Typography by Relish New Brand Experience
Printed in Canada by Friesens

LIBRARY AND ARCHIVES CANADA CATALOGUING IN PUBLICATION

Koller, Katherine, 1957-, author
    Art lessons / Katherine Koller.

Issued in print and electronic formats.

ISBN 978-1-927855-49-2 (paperback).--ISBN 978-1-927855-50-8 (epub).--ISBN 978-1-927855-51-5 (mobi)

    I. Title.

PS8571.O693A89 2016   C813'.54   C2016-902039-8
                                        C2016-902040-1

ENVIRONMENTAL BENEFITS STATEMENT

Great Plains Publications saved the following resources by printing the pages of this book on chlorine free paper made with 100% post-consumer waste.

TREES	WATER	ENERGY	SOLID WASTE	GREENHOUSE GASES
5	2,266	3	151	417
FULLY GROWN	GALLONS	MILLION BTUs	POUNDS	POUNDS

 Environmental impact estimates were made using the Environmental Paper Network Paper Calculator 3.2. For more information visit www.papercalculator.org.

Canada

FSC
www.fsc.org

MIX
Paper from
responsible sources
FSC™ C016245

ACKNOWLEDGEMENTS

Margaret Macpherson and Laurel Sproule, from the beginning, patiently read this novel in pieces. I could not have started or finished without their encouragment and guidance. Zosia Wojcicki graciously provided Polish phrases and spellings. Thoughtful sessions with Betsy Warland were revealing. Joanne Gerber of the Access Copyright Foundation and Helen Humphreys and Margaret Hart at Humber College all provided valuable support. Lisa Moore and the Writing with Style group at The Banff Centre (Fall 2010) gave useful comments, for which I am sincerely grateful. I treasure my discussions about art with artists Nancy Corrigan and Catherine Compston.

"White Woods," was first published under the title "Art Lessons" in *Alberta Views,* September 2011; "Autumn Colours," was first published as "Colour" in *Room* 37.1, Spring 2014; "Tree Day" appeared in *Room* 37.4, Winter 2014; "Hollow Oak" was published in the 2014 *National Voices,* an anthology by the Canadian Authors Association (Vancouver); and "Trees Entwined" appears as "Polish Wedding" in the *Anthology of Canadian-Polish Writing,* published by Guernica Editions in 2017.

With love, always, to my daughters
Hannah Kristin
Elfi Katherine
Monika Starr
Sophie Mariah
Vita Larsen
Rebekah Joy

CONTENTS

1 Yellow Apple Tree 13

2 Enchanted Forest 23

3 Memory Tree 33

4 Forest of Friends 43

5 Baby Tree 51

6 Tree of Heaven 57

7 Family Tree 65

8 Lemon Tree 71

9 Hollow Oak 79

10 Tree Day 87

11 Tree of Abundance 95

12 Evergreen 107

13 Blossoms 113

14 Trees Entwined 121

15 Autumn Colours 133

16 Late Spring Frost 143

17 White Woods 151

18 Heartwood 165

19 Tree of Possibilities 177

To move freely you must be deeply rooted.

Bella Lewitzky, dancer

...enter into the life of the trees. Know your relationship and understand their language, unspoken, unwritten talk....

So, artist, you too from the deeps of your soul, down among dark and silence, let your roots creep forth, gaining strength.... Rejoice in your own soil, the place that nurtured you when a helpless seed.

Emily Carr, *Hundreds and Thousands*

YELLOW APPLE TREE

I HUG BABCI'S WAIST. Her high heels stab the old wood floors and my socks slide, shuffling from her bedroom down the hall to the living room. Laughing, she pulls me off like a piece of thread stuck to her stocking, checking her packing, the gifts she's taking, her passport, funny Polish money in faded purple, orange and green, her ticket. Her purse has a clear plastic covering over pink and yellow embroidered flowers. At the bottom of that purse there are hard candies with chewy fruit centres wrapped in folded white papers with plums, cherries or limes. I want one. Babci always has Polish candies for me.

Not now, she says. Babci pinches that purse closed, a sharp, metal click.

My hand wings back, and knocks a tall wooden spool. It clatters and rolls under the dining room table. Gold thread unravels in the dust balls against the wall. I stoop under the table and wind it slowly and evenly, finding the notch in the wood for the end of the thread, jamming it in tight. The thread breaks. I fit the thread in its slot again. My Babci is in a hurry. To go away. Without me. Click.

Babci doesn't even like to be away. She won't stay overnight at our house because, she says, my angels need me. She keeps candles burning day and night for her angels in her bedroom.

When I told Daddy, he put a smoke detector in there. Then, also at Auntie Magda's when Mommy said Auntie Magda almost burned down her condo. A birthday card from Babci:

To my pearl Magda, wish you love. It caught fire, at night, from a lit candle. Auntie Magda hoped the angels' breath in the candle would open Babci's heart to Auntie Magda's new boyfriend, who was married before. Instead, it burned a hole in Auntie Magda's fuchsia fringed scarf.

Babci zigzag sewed it so you could not see. She blamed the boyfriend.

He's second hand clothes, said Babci. Why second hand when you can have brand new?

Why go to Poland when you can go to the mountains?

The only time Babci goes anywhere I go, too, to Miette Hot Springs. Puffy Polish ladies soak and yak and watch me dive in the hot pool, then the cool pool, then back to the hot steam. I pretend I'm flying in the steamy air, floating on top of the water, with the tall mountain trees all around. In the eensy log cabin, Babci feeds me cabbage rolls with kapusta and tomato sauce and I tumble into a hide-a-bed that muffles the sad laughter of ladies with little knives and muscley thumbs peeling Babci's apples.

The day Babci let me pick the first apple, the lowest one, I bit into it, but it wasn't really ready yet. It tasted green and sour. I made a face at Babci.

I go to my sister. Your big Ciocia.

But she's not big. We saw her picture. And she's younger. Your little sister.

Big Ciocia is your great aunt, says Mom. My auntie. Like Babci's mother was my Babci. Your big Babci.

You never even knew your own Babci. How can you let mine go?

Babci's only going on a little trip, Mom says.

Can I go, too?

Oh, little birdie. Babci's eyes sparkle. Not you.

I throw the first apple into the street. Babci shakes her head.

Nie, nie, she says, like when a dress or a suit doesn't fit quite right. I watch the apple roll and get smushed by a truck. The apples aren't even yellow yet! Neither are the leaves. When the apples are sweet, thin-skin buttery yellow, I eat ten a day.

Daddy and Charlie and Tom pick all the high apples on the ladder. I only get to pick the low ones, and the ones on the ground. Babci and Mom cut and chop them for freezing. Stella squeezes lemon juice on them and stuffs them in plastic bags.

Mom says even if Babci says yes, she says no.

I can miss some of Grade Two! I liked Grade One better. Can't I go? Mom?

It's too far and too long, Cassie.

Today I bounced in before Babci's screen door could spank me, and Babci said hello, hello, but no little birdie, no hug, no cheek pinching, no chance for me to ask pretty please can I go, too. And no candies.

I thought I was one of her angels.

The first time she showed me, in her bedroom, her little altar covered in doily cloth, her tall candles in jars, she said, I all the time thinking of you.

This is why she keeps her candles lit, so the angels are always there. Angels keep up your prayer, she says, when your hands are busy.

Mom uses patterns by *Butterick* and *Simplicity* and *McCall's*. But Babci's ladies bring her magazines like *People* and *Life* to get the outfit in the pictures. Like a coatdress in the style of Jackie O who used to be Jackie K, Mom says. But I know why Babci can make anything she sees. Because of her angels.

When I was three I had water wings to hold me up in the pool. But when I do my art, I float by myself. I call it being on a cloud.

The first time I am four. Stella is a new baby. Mommy is with Stella a lot. I'm drawing at my own table in the sunroom. It feels the same as floating. Mommy sits on the carpet. In a sunbeam. Her blue shirt shines. I draw that sunny sky blue, and her different long hair browns. I use five pencil crayons to make her hair *stripeys*. And then I have to touch it. She catches me when I come down from my desk.

Click, she says. I took a picture of you!

Where's your camera?

In my head. Click. In my memory bank.

I wrap a bracelet of Mommy's hair smooth and shiny on my arm.

My arms are lonely for you, she says.

There's baby spit on the shoulder of her blue shirt so I curl under her neck spot that still fits my head.

Under my wingtip, she says.

Her hand rests on my head. I sniff her baby milk shirt. I love that Mommy smell.

Now Mom pulls me out from under Babci's table. I slam the big spool back upright in the middle of the table. Mom keeps my hand and folds her tennis skirt carefully under her on the edge of the couch. She sits me down on her lap because I'm wearing shorts and Babci's couch feels like dry Bran Flakes. Mom took me out of school after her tennis game while Stella is at playschool so I can say goodbye to Babci to the airport.

Mom waits until Babci is running water in the bath for her plants. Then she whispers in my ear.

Cassie, make sure the candles are O-U-T! Mom and I spell words so Stella and Louis the dog don't get it. Babci doesn't spell English words very well, either.

Babci's bedroom smells like Jergens. Babci says almonds and cherries but I think it smells like her. I squirt some out. There is one candle still flickering: the red one, in a pickle jar, for Dziadziu, my grandpa in his grave. The huge Jergens bottle always gobs out too much, so I rub the lotion on my knees, except for the scabby parts, and tell Dziadziu to watch over Babci. Or else she might come back with a Polish boyfriend like her friend Gisella, who phones Babci every day. And every day she says the same thing. The boyfriend only married Gisella to come to Canada and open a video store and smoke cigars and argue in Polish with the old men at Christmas parties and then he left her.

So much for Solidarity, Mom said.

Babci wants a good husband for Ciocia Magda, one who is handsome, handy and holy, but I wonder if she wants a new one of her own. She laughs and says Ciocia Magda also needs a tall one, to reach the light bulb and the smoke detector, like Daddy.

Babci wears a navy blue suit, smart like in *Vogue*. She knows how to make her clothes fit to show her waist and put makeup and jewelry on. Not too many points or it's gauche, like Mom says. Babci is pink and out of breath in the hallway, the way Auntie Magda is when she's getting ready for a date.

I blow out the red Dziadziu candle. I wave my hands in the lacey smoke, except I don't pray at it in Polish like Babci does. Babci click-steps into the bedroom, hurrying her Polish whispers, then shoos me out and shuts the door quick behind her to keep the angels in there. And Dziadziu.

When she's gone back to the kitchen I open the bedroom door a crack so Dziadziu can get out and watch her step. No new boyfriend for Babci! I hardly ever get to see Auntie Magda because she either drives her car selling houses or goes out with boyfriends. But if Auntie Magda ever goes away to find a tall Polish husband who is handsome, handy and holy, I will teach him English. Daddy hung up a big blackboard that fits across a whole wall in our basement, and I teach Stella her animal and insect words with chalk. I draw them and she says them.

Last year Miss Trepanier taught me French. Each time you answer her French question she comes over and gives you a little touch on your arm or your shoulder or your head, to keep the answer in. Her touches are like sunbeams. She smells like lemonade. She smiles and makes us smile all day.

Comment-allez vous?

Très bien, Madamoiselle.

Moi aussi, parce que je suis chez nous!

Each afternoon when the children went home, Miss Trepanier closed the Grade One porte to keep the goodness in. I think she meant her goodness. Mom says classroom doors must be closed in case of fire. But every time Miss Trepanier closed the door and hugged me goodbye and limped down the long hallway with Mr. Cane, I stayed behind, and j'ai ouvré la porte encore a teeny bit. So her goodness could get out and I could feel it wherever I go. I even feel it now, just thinking about her, her arm on the back of my neck, her sunny lemon perfume.

Because Babci's busy emptying her fridge, I sneak-sit on the coffee table in front of the ouchy couch. The picture on the wall behind is *The Last Supper* when Jesus says goodbye to his friends. Mom brings in bags and bags of yummy leftovers to take home and I slide onto her lap again.

Why does Babci have to go?

Babci was only seventeen when she left Poland, Mom says.

I'm seven. Seventeen is old.

Forty years ago. That's a long time to miss your parents, your sister, your cousins and all the new children in the family, Mom is saying.

So the candies are for them.

Babci will be back in forty days. A day for each year she was gone. Right, Cassie?

Daddy is forty!

So am I, almost.

Do you want to go to Poland? Mom?

She pulls out a pack of gum from her floppy smooth red leather bag.

Not without you. Or Daddy and the boys and Stella.

I break the stick of Juicy Fruit gum in half like Daddy always does. Then I try to join the halves together again but I can't. I bet Freddy could.

I think I'll marry Freddy. He's my best friend from kindergarten. Babci won't have to go away to Poland to find a husband for me. Freddy likes our house because the boys have lots of Lego. Freddy builds *skyreachers* and brings his own yellow flag piece for the top. Charlie and Tommy crash through their Lego like waves, but Freddy sharp I-spies what he needs and picks it up quietly while I draw. Once he broke my black crayon trying to write on white Lego. But he right away fixed it with tape. If Freddy talks when we play it's short.

Where do you go, Cassie?

Up. Like your skyreacher.

On the stairs or an elevator?

I lift up by myself. I hear your flag flapping.

And then we get back to our own beeswax.

Freddy's mother married a new father and Freddy moved away. One day he will come back and marry me.

When Babci leaves us at the airport line-up, I make Mom wait. I keep my eyes on Babci in the slow snake of people. I want her to see my arm waving in my quilted yellow jacket she made me, yellow like Freddy's flag. I even do some pretend whispers to see if she can hear my angel talk: Ch-zy-clk-co szia.

Mom lifts me up and Babci turns and shakes her white hanky and her eyes smile at me and I wave and wave until Mom pulls me away. Outside, I watch her airplane take off. Babci is very brave. It's her first airplane. But she has her rosary working, praying with her angels.

I take Mom's hand so I can bend way back to look up and see the line the airplane makes. Daddy goes in airplanes all the time to work up North. It's like sitting in your living room, he said to Babci. She came to Canada on a boat. When I draw, I go higher than Freddy's skyreachers, but not as high as Babci's airplane.

Even from the van I can still hear the zoom of the airplane and I hope Babci plugs her ears. I can hear her in my head, Zdrowaś Maryjo, saying her beads. On the ride home, I stare out at the fields, looking for trees watching, waiting for Babci to come back.

Mom leaves me in the van while she runs to get Stella at playschool. She tells me to look in the glove compartment. There's a sketchbook with a hard cover, like a real book. It fits in my yellow jacket pocket. There's a pencil, too, a short one with a still-good eraser that fits in the other pocket. It even has the date pencilled in by Mom: September 6, 1987. This book is my forty-day book. I wear my yellow jacket every one of those days, even when it snows before Halloween.

I write a story with a picture of Babci and some writing on each page.

> <u>Babci, Come Home</u>
> Light your candles.
> Take the plants out of your bathtub.
> Plug in your tiny TV.
> Fill up your fridge with sour cream and Root Beer.
> Make your sewing machine run speedy and happy.
> Make apple szarlotka, crispy and crumbly.
> Give the extra crumbs to your birds.
> Talk to your angels.

I colour the pictures with my new pastel set. Mom says the pastels are big girl crayons like oil paint is grownup paint. Only eight colours and they break if you drop them. I use sharp pencil crayons over the words and every letter is a different colour in order of blue, yellow, green, orange, purple and red. Freddy likes colour order, too. He goes from white to black, lightest to darkest, but I like mixing mine.

Mom says, if you're cranky, go draw.

So I do. I draw every day to stay floating, like Babci's angels. They work on her prayers and I work on my Babci book. When I get to the end, my yellow flag jacket is not so yellow anymore, like apples left at the top of the tree for the winter birds.

ENCHANTED FOREST

IT'S TIME, SHE SAYS.

Mom sits down on the sofa beside my sunroom desk. I unplug my glue gun, the best eighth birthday present ever. I leave my creation not quite done, but I'll finish it at lunch. It's a windmill, like in Holland, like in the book the principal, Mr. Daniels, is reading us in the library. I'm making it with a moving wheel from cut-up toilet paper rolls. I need to paint it. Orange?

Hurry up. The boys...

And they grab Orange Crush pop cans, whooping like they just scored, and scoop up two-dollar bills: a Dad lunch today. Usually there's a pile of sandwiches and squares and chocolate milk for them to take, junior high athlete food, but today there's none. The boys shoulder-hit and down bananas and toast-to-go, peanut butter dripping down the sleeves of their half-on jean jackets. Mom doesn't stand up.

Dad splash-fills his mug, takes a giant gulp and leans down to coffee-kiss Mom on his way out.

I'll take them for cleats as soon as I get home, he says. Then burgers. Take it easy. Call me later.

Coffee makes her gag, the smell of it. And burgers, even the word.

Mom uses her elbow to feel her way down on the sofa, then lands her head and pulls her feet up. It's only morning, but the tummy baby has eaten up all her energy already. It doesn't like people food yet. Mom and Dad told the boys and

Stella and me about the new baby on Valentine's Day. Mom can only nibble crackers. And sip warm water.

But I'm starving, so I eat up my Shreddies quick and get back to my desk. I wonder if a tack would work better for my pinwheel and if I can find one—

You're going to have to walk Stella today, Mom says low, like the tummy baby is listening. I don't want Stella to make you late, so check on her? Bring her home at lunch, too.

But my hands are full.

Mom tries to fine-line a smile on her too-tight face. I let the sweaty centres of my pinwheel flap open and stomp upstairs to get Stella ready for kindergarten.

At lunch, Stella is a little faster walking home in the slush because she's hungry. She didn't eat her Corn Flakes because I made them too milky. And I wouldn't make her more, because then she'd get spoiled. I need to eat lunch quick and get back for *The Wheel on the School* at library time and she gets to watch "The Flintstones," but I still have to pull her along. As Mom says, Stella distracts easy. Any slushy puddle, every little bird, each interesting stick. But in the alley we smell grilled cheese sandwiches and Stella rushes ahead because that means Babci is there.

Where's Mom?

They're checking her up.

At the hospital?

You go after school. With Daddy.

Is it the baby?

No worry about that. Eat you lunch.

Stella has two of Babci's buttery crisp sandwiches dunked in ketchup. I give her my second one when Babci's not looking, *girl cheese* Stella calls them, and go to my desk. I clear the pinwheel out of the way for later and fold some paper for a card. I want to draw a Dutch stork like Mr. Daniels showed us in *The Wheel on the School,* but I saw a real robin on the way home and that's a sign of spring. Mom likes birds. She keeps her bird feeder full in the winter, but now it's empty. Mine is a skinny robin, but I make its tummy extra red. It reminds me of her. How it pecks at the ground, like Mom bites her little crackers, so the tummy baby won't notice.

Babci is talking to Stella. Eat you good lunch. Eat, eat! In case you lost in the woods!

But up in my cloud, concentrating on my card, I hear Babci say it to my robin. Eat, eat! My robin looks for worms and can't find any, so she hop-flies to a patch of brown grass left by the snow. You can see her orange-red belly and how hard she is trying. I wonder how she finds her worm. How can she see them under the ground? Does she listen to know where they are? But she's hungry so she has to keep going. She might have babies to feed.

I used to think the woods in Babci's talk were a magic, enchanted forest, until I got lost. I keep drawing to stay up and float, because I sink if I think about it. I keep marking feathers on my robin with my charcoal pencil, to not be lost in the woods.

Only Stella still says Mommy. When I got lost I was six and Mom was Mommy.

On my walk home from school, my skipping rope is a tail. Down the long block of houses of people I don't know. Past the spy tree. The grumpy sky wants to burp. I skip my rope now, slow and slappy to make the rain burst.

The lines in the sidewalk are fences and I'm a horse jumping high. Green and yellow gardens grow in the cracks.

Snap-a-swish-swish, my pink rainbow rope goes, sweeping the wind.

My jumps are just right. I'm keeping the beat, and if I step on a crack, I don't break anyone's back. No, and I don't need that stick-stick-stick ticker Mommy bought for the piano, either, because I'm good at the beat now. Miss Trepanier said. She plays violin to the Grade Ones when we need a rest. Mr. Bow flows like the seaweed inside our class aquarium. Miss Trepanier says to count bouncing bubbles in my head, like she does with her violin, to keep my piano fingers on time. I don't like the gnome in the metronome. Sometimes Charlie and Tommy put it on presto and play machine gun with it when Mommy is in the backyard digging carrots.

Run the skinny sidewalk, up the four steps, swing the screen wide, and... the front door is locked. I ring the doorbell, slam hard on the door with my hand and... no one's there.

The sky looks growly. Not burpy anymore, but mad. The stinky yellow and orange daisy flowers on the side of the house are dangly. They close up without the sun.

The back door, locked, too. Louis sleeps in his doghouse and doesn't even get up. My ropey tail drags in the yellows and rips one out. I pick up the flower and pull out each skinny yellow petal. The curtains, closed. I sit on the front steps.

She loves me, she loves me not, I sing, louder than the wind. Where is Mommy?

The sky wants to cry.

I wrap my pink skipping rope around my waist, and tie one end to the railing. I make a desk with my knees and fold my arms on it and put my head down for a rest, like Miss Trepanier always says after recess. I go to my *memory bank* and listen. I listen for her voice, for her violin, but I'm hungry.

My skipping rope under my shoe is a giant spit-out string of bubblegum.

Miss Trepanier says read if you're hungry so the time will trot until snacks. I look in the mailbox.

There's a magazine, *Chat-Elaine*. Miss Trepanier has a French name, too. Chat is for cat. And Elaine is a girl. We have Elaine in our class. She's quiet, like a cat. But no cats here, just ladies and perfume. There's a tear-off one, and I open it, because Mommy always lets me have them. It's pee-yew, like chat-pee.

There's some letters for Dad, Mr. David Penn. Two Ns just because. Like a pen that writes dark with no goobers or missed spots, a good pen. We only use fat pencils for printing in Grade One. I wish our name had a Y. Then I'd be a Penny. A lucky Penny.

I look again and there's also a little pink letter in the mailbox and it's for ...Miss Kasia Penn! 9020-145 Street, Edmonton, Alberta. Only Babci calls me Kasia. I can tell her writing, swirly and standing straight up. The stamp is queen blue. Babci loves the queen like I love Miss Trepanier. Babci has a picture of the queen with her crown on, in a blue coat, the same royal blue as the one Babci made me this year for Easter. And one for my doll Rosa, with white satin lining and a matching blue bonnet that ties under her baby chin. Stella loves Rosa.

It's my first mail. Inside the envelope is a shining Jesus with sparkles on it. For my little birdie. Easter Blessings 1987. Love and kisses from Babci. My finger gets sparkles on it. I wipe them on my forehead like Jesus, to be lucky like him, because he didn't die. And so I sparkle like a penny. I put the card back in the little pink envelope and close it. Then take it out and read it some more.

I'm Babci's birdie except I can't fly because I'm tied to the railing and the stinky perfume is on my fingers and I wipe my eyes and they sting and the tears spill out.

Mommy opens the door.

Cassie, there you are!

Where were you?

I was on the phone, honey.

But I rang the doorbell!

I came to the door, but no one was here! I thought it was a knock-a-door Ginger!

The back door was locked, too!

I just got home, and put Stella down for her nap. I forgot to unlock the doors.

I give her the mail, but not mine. She unties my rope. My heart beats quick. We have a little hug. There are grocery bags all over the floor of the kitchen.

Was it Daddy?

Mr. Daniels.

What for?

Miss Trepanier is sick.

I know. We had a sub today a-gain!

He says Miss Trepanier is so sick that she can't come back to teach.

Why?

It would be too hard.

She says we can do anything if we try. She says I don't have to stop, point and check anymore at silent reading. She says I'm engrossed.

I know. I love her, too. But she needs to go to the hospital.

How could she be so sick? She's not even married yet. She's a Miss, like me. She has the best shiny smile. And she has soft sweaters and hugs. Mr. Cane, her helper, comes to school. He's wooden, with a hook to go on her chair. He comes out for recess with her to hold her up. She wears scarves to keep her head warm. Even inside. She gets coughs. She sips cinnamon tea.

Is she going to say goodbye?

She is sending a letter to the class. And the class will write one to her.

And draw pictures?

Yes. Mr. Daniels said she especially asked for one from you.

Miss Trepanier touches you on the back of your neck like she's poking her sun smile into your head, giving your brain some light, so that's what I draw. Even though I can't see her I feel her sun. When I float, her sun reaches me.

I wish Miss Trepanier could have waited for Freddy to grow up to be a genius so he could fix her, but Miss Trepanier is one of my angels now.

I find a robin-egg blue envelope from Mom's desk drawer and put in my robin card and lick it closed.

Dad takes us all for hamburgers on the way to the hospital.

Babci prays her pearly pink rosary the whole way, even at the A & W drive-in, sipping her baby root beer, which is all she ever gets. She only eats her own food to keep her waist. Babci says, for women, no matter what's on top and bottom, only have a waist.

Charlie and Tommy wear their new cleats to get used to them. They are in French fry heaven. The car smells of sweaty runners and onion rings. The boys beg for my last half of hamburger so I rip it in two pieces.

Then we drop off Babci. She says, I have my sewing now.

Babci hates the hospital, because Dziadziu died there. I was really little because I don't remember. When Stella was born, Mom got stitches on her tummy. That's the only time I went to the hospital. I never got to go when Miss Trepanier was there. Mom said no. Babci didn't go the time Mom was there with Stella, either. Instead, she had hot borscht and sour cream and crusty buns ready when we got home.

Daddy takes the boys to Emergency when they get hurt, to stitch up knees and lips and chins. They take the stitching day off but go back to playing their sports the next day. Mom can't watch the boys get stitches. Neither could I. They keep count of their stitches so far: Charlie has nine and Tommy has twelve.

Dad helps Babci out of the van and promises to phone her from the hospital. Babci doesn't stop her praying the whole time. One hand has her beads, the other her key, and I don't wave either.

My hand sweats on my card because it is hot as a swimming pool in the hospital. The air makes my head heavy. In the bed, Mom hardly moves. Just her eyes and mouth.

The baby came out before it was ready, she says. It wasn't growing right, like a cake that flops.

My tummy flips. I lean against the high bed.

Tommy butts in. Was it a boy?

Not really a baby yet. It was a miss.

I'm a miss. I'm Miss Cassie Penn.

No, Daddy says, lifting me on to the bed. Like a soccer goal you miss.

Like a mistake, says Tommy.

Charlie starts to bump him. Daddy takes the boys and Stella to get some cold water for Mom and to phone Babci.

Any stitches? I ask.

No stitches. You can look.

Mom tries to pull down the covers, but her arm is too sleepy, so I do it. I pat her tummy. It's not stretched like before. It's soft and squishy.

What's a miss?

A miscarriage. Lots of mommies have one.

I cover her back up and open the blue envelope for her to hold the card I made.

It's a robin looking for the enchanted forest. For the other robins.

So spring is here?

Not really. This robin came too early. Like the miss.

Oh, and one big tear drips down from Mom. I catch it with the scrunchy sheet.

I look at the hungry robin again. It's got me in it, because I made it, and it's got Mom, because it's for her. But there's something else in it that only we can see. The miss.

MEMORY TREE

MOM STAYS ON THE phone a lot. She makes the boys' lunches and even puts Old Dutch BBQ potato chips in. When she goes into the bathroom, she cries. She's put my robin card in a purple wood frame on the wall behind the mirror, so it peeks behind you when you brush your teeth. I wonder if the robin makes her cry.

It knows how I feel, Mom says.

She starts making quilts. She makes a Log Cabin one for our sunroom, for Daddy's little naps on the couch. She makes a Heart one for Auntie Magda, a Pine Tree for me and a Sunflower Sue for Stella. She sews all summer long, and even takes her sewing machine outside and Daddy plugs it in with an extension cord. I like looking at her pattern books, and helping her decide about colours. She wants to make a Star of Bethlehem to put on Babci's ouchy couch, a Blue Birds of Happiness for our kitchen, and a Wild Goose Chase for the TV room on winter nights. Charlie and Tom surprise her when they say they want quilts, too. She thinks she'll make matching Log Cabin designs, because the boys think they look like bulls' eyes, in blue for Charlie and purple for Tom. I hint she should make them both in browns to match, because of the boys' muddy jeans, with accents of blue for Charlie and bits of purple for Tom. And red for the centres of the log cabin blocks. And she does.

I have a bigger sketchbook now, as big as my Grade Four Duo-Tangs. Daddy and I went to the art store. It's a jumble of every kind of art supply you could imagine stacked up on tall shelves. I'm like Daddy in Canadian Tire when I'm at the art store, in a kind of drooly daze. The art store guy, a real artist with a long grey ponytail, uses a black hard-covered sketchbook. He shows how the coil binding opens better to lie flat. He makes charcoal drawings of horses. Only horses. I buy new charcoal sticks with my own money. Daddy also buys me the coil black sketchbook and a small notebook for my idea. I'm making a special minibook for Mom. I'm going to use charcoal sticks for drawings and black fine liner for the words. The charcoal is okay for the ants and the seashells, but doing whole people is too much, so I just do the hands. Charcoal works for close-up drawing, especially for shells and balls. And hands. I do the action with my left hand while I draw it with the right one. The pages go in this order:

> Feel Better List for Mom
> Throw your crumbs outside for the ants.
> Make your honey lentil soup.
> Wash your seashells.
> Read. Your book, not a magazine.
> Feed the dog.
> Play ball with the boys.
> Make tea and toast with your crabapple jelly.
> Stitch your quilting.
> Sneak some chocolate chips with your girls.
> Flap your sheets in the wind.

I show Mom my pages and her hands are wet from the sink and some drops land on the sheet in the wind page and make the sheet blurry, like it's moving. I splatter it some more with spit, but drips of water work better. Mom dries her hands and sits down with my pages. She's got a smile on, finally. I ask if she can sneak the chocolate chips out of their hiding place but she won't. Not now. She's getting us ready.

Today Daddy's taking the boys to a basketball tournament in Red Deer overnight, so Stella and I get to go on a holiday to Babci's. Mom's getting a day off from us.

Stella puts pink Barbie bubbles in Mom's bath and I bring Mom her *Chatelaine*. Mom says it means like a queen, not a cat. In the steamy bathroom, I tell Miss Trepanier in my mind that she is une belle ange and my mom is la chatelaine forte. I take out the perfume cards from the magazine so they don't get wet and wave them around the steaminess so it smells better than Barbie bubbles. Daddy pours Mom a little glass of something darker and stinkier than wine and puts the dog out and we go.

Daddy drives without ever stopping. He gets green lights like prizes all the way. He drives relaxed and happy and listens to a talk show on the radio, it never matters what. He listens and laughs. I'm in the front seat. Driving with Daddy in the dark puts me in dreamland. The boys actually quit punching each other, like they're a bit hypnotized. Stella sleeps bundled up between them in the back, letting out little puffs.

It takes a long time to drive downtown to Babci's, but finally we turn at the gravestone store. You can see the different shapes and colours of gravestones, and they have writing on them. It's too dark to read it, but the writing makes me wonder. Did those people order them and then, not die? Or not pay? Or forget to have someone pick them up? I wonder if you can miss dying like Jesus, who pushed away his tombstone, way bigger than a gravestone. I wonder if you can miss dying like you can miss getting born.

When we're almost at Babci's, the car slows down and my heart speeds up. The boys start slapping each other again. Stella and I get out, with our knapsacks and our dolls, and Daddy gives us some quarters to spend. Babci kisses us, my little birdie to me, honeybunch to Stella. Even the boys let her because she's holding a steamy cup of coffee for Daddy and three paper bags of warm cinnamon sugar-dusted homemade doughnuts.

Then it's just the girls and Babci and the fairy light of her tiny TV. We cuddle up each side of her, wrapped carefully in our quilts on the ouchy couch. I check for leftover dressmaking pins lined up over Babci's heart on her burgundy dress and stick them to the big black magnet on her coffee table. We each have a plate with two doughnuts and eat them slowly, licking up every single crumb. Babci changes channels, looking for a show with singing or dancing or skating. Babci likes anybody with sequins, like Elton John. Tonight it's Cher. Babci likes her, but says she's too skinny and invites her to come have some doughnuts and we laugh. After, Babci played her Liberace tape again on our old video machine Daddy set up. Babci loves Liberace because he's Polish. But his glissando piano playing makes me and Stella fall asleep. At the end, Babci wakes us up with her clapping.

We phone Mom before we go to bed.

Are you lonesome, Mommy? Stella says. I listen on the phone.

I've got the dog, and I'm making something pretty ...

She's playing her "Bridge over Troubled Waters" really loud, so I can't really hear.

Goodnight, Mom!

Sleep tight!

We climb in the cloud bed, under the satin feather comforter that sounds like queen robes and has a sheen like red and gold sunset. It smells like doughnuts under there, because Babci puts them in the bed to keep them warm when they come out of the oven. When the light is off, we count in Polish. I say it, then Stella does.

Jeden. Jeden.

Dwa. Dwa.

Trzy. Trzy.

We never get to five, which sounds like pinch!

In the morning Babci takes thick airy honey toast out of the oven in her creaky little kitchen, all warm and wooden. Then we play while she sews for her ladies. She shows us the outfits she's making so we can pick fabrics for our Barbies.

Babci sews and sews and sews in her workroom and comes out with something almost finished. We spy on her. Her birds chirp in the bushes under the corner windows and her teeny radio plays tinny music. The sewing room smells like new fabric and metal and sewing machine oil and the damp of the ironing board.

Go play. I working now.

I say that exact same thing, the same way, to Stella when I'm doing my art, at home, and she listens to me because she's heard Babci say it.

Babci gives us a shoebox of scraps and scissors and needles and thread, and we sew what we can. We dress our Barbies in strips, making little tied-on ragged skirts and pinned-on shawls and balled-up hats. Then Babci, like the night mice in *The Tailor of Gloucester,* takes our designs and finishes them overnight. The next morning, we have matching ball gowns with sequins on top and long flowing velvet below. Mine is deep green and Stella's is midnight blue. Our dolls look like Cher. Mom will pretend to be jealous because she never had Barbies, but Babci made all of Mom's tap dancing costumes and we get to use them at Babci's for dress-up.

After lunch we go down the alley, through a skinny board-walk between two old yards of tall weeds to the candy store on the next street. Babci calls it the Chinaman store, but the man in the white moustache and dark blue flat cap talks like the Queen. The candy is in red packages with Chinese writing. The man puts our candies in a little white paper bag, one for each of us, smoothing them with his whole hand, like Daddy used to touch Stella's head when she was a baby. I ask the man if he has any grandchildren. His eyes go watery and he holds up three fingers and says, China. Then he puts a chocolate gold coin in each of our bags for good luck. We remember to say thank you like Babci said and we run all the way back.

While Babci steam-presses her work from the morning, we're supposed to water each plant in the garden with a bucket and a ladle: two ladles for tomatoes and one for everything else. It takes five buckets and Babci watches from her window, where the ironing board stands. I water while Stella mostly looks for worms and bugs and talks to Mrs. Sekula over the fence that leans backwards and forwards. Babci tells us not to touch the fence in case it falls down on someone. Mrs. Sekula can't really speak English, but she and Stella compare insects over the wavy fence. They look at a bud on her apple tree, and Mrs. Sekula shows how the bud will open like her fist, into a finger flower and then a round apple. Stella makes her smile. I like Mrs. Sekula's smile because she's missing her front teeth but she does it anyway.

Babci won't let us watch TV with her in the afternoon. We peeked once, and it was all whispery talking. And yucky kissing. Babci likes it to learn her English. Mom says it's called soap opera and Babci never skips a day.

Now is my story. Go play.

She does her hand-sewing at the TV and we are not allowed to go in her bedroom to look at the angel candles so we go upstairs, where she used to have boarders, to explore. There were people living in the basement, too, when she had Dziadziu. I only remember him from his pictures and his gravestone, pure black, the same as his hair. In the honey-coloured hope chest upstairs, we find Mom's old school work wrapped in carmel tissue pattern sheets. I want to keep the pencil drawings of ruby flowers, shaded and outlined like from an old-fashioned library book, and Stella wants the big one of a ladybug, but no, Babci says, those are no for you. Stella gets ready to wail, so I show her how to trace it in the window while she holds it up. Then I make Stella colour it herself, and it's not at all like Mom's in the end but Stella loves it.

I want to phone Mom to ask her about her drawings but Babci won't let me.

Leave her a little bit lonely today.

Babci says lonely like it is as normal and natural as growing. I tell her about being lonely on the steps at home that time the door was locked, and how her sparkly Easter card saved me, and she holds both my hands and says it's my turn to send her something. Babci loves getting mail. She reads her Polish mail at night, in bed, with her glasses and a big ahhh as she slits the envelope with a little knife on her night table. She reads aloud, so her Dzaidziu angel can hear. I promise that if I ever go anywhere, I will send Babci a postcard.

Babci has a whole box of postcards, from when she was young and alone in Canada. She lets us play with them. We try to figure out where they are from by the stamps. *Polska* is easy but others are not. Some are from African countries and Argentina. The writing stands up tall and curly like Babci's and all of it is Polish.

Babci teaches us Polish while she's cooking fried potatoes and pork chops and making creamy sweet lettuce salad. We clean out her spice cupboard. She says it, then we say it.

Dobry. Good.

Lalka. Doll.

Mleko. Milk.

We sniff in each spice jar like Babci does when she uses them. There are no labels, so we put them in colour order, lightest to darkest.

White garlic salt.

Yellow mustard powder.

Orange paprika.

Green dill weed.

Brown cloves.

Black pepper.

When Daddy comes to pick us up it is already night.

We carry bags of food to take home: leftover angel-food cake with rhubarb sauce from Babci and my favourite, sauerkraut carrot kapusta and Ukrainian sausage from Mrs. Sekula, for you mama. There is also a secret bag of boys' jeans with the knees mended so invisible that the boys don't even notice when they put them on.

I wave until Babci shrinks to a wiggly dot on the road behind us. On the way home I don't see the gravestone store. On my side of the car, I get the glow and smoke and the fry smell of the A & W and settle into the sleepy quiet of the dark drive. Suddenly home, the lights glare. Louis wags his tail as he sits quietly beside Mom, who's wearing something from *Glamour,* probably, with makeup and a new perfume.

Mom bustles us to bed, oohing at our new doll clothes and aahing at the scores the boys made. Daddy turns off the lights. While Mom says goodnight to us, Daddy lights a new green candle at the kitchen table. He doesn't even grumble about it, but puts a saucer under it to catch the wax. It smells like pinecones. Later I hear them drinking tea. Louis lands like a rug under the table. I try to listen to their talking, but all I hear is Stella's little-sigh breathing in the bunk bed above me and the boys snoring in the next room and the running hum of Babci's sewing machine, smoothly, surely, sewing up our seams.

FOREST OF FRIENDS

MOM'S BAKING COOKIES. But not for us.

You can always tell when the cookies are to give away because she doesn't give out the spatula for anyone to lick. She gets red in the face and stamps her foot when the boys scoop their fingers in the dough and take a big hunk, running out the door before she can swat them with a dishtowel. There are raw eggs in cookie dough, so I don't ever eat it. But the boys don't care. They eat everything.

They're boys, says Mom, often. Human garburators.

When I'm mad at them, Mom says there will come a time when you will be very interested in boys. I don't know. The only boy I ever liked so far is Freddy, since I was four. But he moved away to a new school.

I suck in the oatsy chocolate aroma of the cookies baking and try to hold in the goodness, but sadness pricks through. My friend Annie is moving, too. Mom is making cookies for Annie, Annie's baby brother Ben and their mom. They're moving today. The dad already moved, to somewhere else, with a new lady who is having her own baby. Annie and her mom and Ben are going to the small town where her Granny lives. Annie's Granny has frizzled grey hair falling down from the top of her head. She has a big smile of clicking false teeth and says for me to call her Granny, too. She visits a lot. Granny loves holding baby Ben and taking him for walks. She says she's an outside girl. She has a suntan even in winter and likes to play basketball with us. And when the boys want to play, too, she makes us stay and be on her team, girls against boys. The boys get baby Ben. So if he cries or needs his soother, the boys have to do something about it and then Granny passes to us, we shoot and the girls usually get a point. We won three games!

The driveway is finally dry of snow. Before, when you missed the ball it landed in the slushy alley puddles. Now I only have Charlie and Tom to play with, but they hardly ever let me have the ball. I only get it if it runs down the alley. They don't stop calling at me until I bring it back.

The cookies are for the long drive away. No nuts because of baby Ben. Granny says he's got a sniffer like a smart dog, and no one can hide a cookie from him. He wails like his finger is caught in a door if he doesn't have two cookies, one in each hand. Granny always puts the baby under the apple tree for naps, and his little nose wiggles when the snowflakes fall and the wind whispers on his cheek. It breathes on him like Granny blows on his hot cereal, and his eyes flutter closed and his mouth drops open. Catching flies, Granny says.

Mom's making the cookies extra crispy so Ben can gnaw on them all the way to Vulcan. It sounds like a scary place, but Annie says it isn't. Granny knows every single person who lives there and everyone calls her Granny. They're driving right after the leftovers lunch that they're eating right now on the porch. The movers have already taken everything away.

Annie doesn't think she'll see her dad very much anymore. She's pretty sad about that. If I couldn't see my dad, nothing would make sense. Days and nights would be mixed up, like on a different hemisphere. At least baby Ben will have Granny to teach him basketball. Even though her mom says they'll visit, Annie doesn't think so. She's moved before. We could write letters, Mom says, be pen pals. I tried that with Miss Trepanier, and she never got a chance to write me back. But Annie says for sure she will write to me. She promised.

Freddy still writes to me. He sends me a birthday card every year and I send him one I've drawn myself, because we're twins. Not like his twin sisters from a different daddy who is black, but because we have the same birthday and are the same age every August 3. Our moms met in the hospital. He sends cards by famous artists, even from when we were five.

I still have the first card, with Vincent van Gogh, *Vase of Roses,* on the front and Hppy Birday, Your frend, Freddy, on the back. I keep all of Freddy's cards.

Freddy gets me. Mom keeps track of his address from his mother who moved to Toronto. They phone each other and have laughing talks. Freddy and I will keep sending cards to each other because we are the oldest friends each other has. Freddy moved to Toronto for a while, but then he went to Geneva, Switzerland.

He now lives with his real dad, a famous scientist who travels around the world, so Freddy goes to private school. I asked him what it feels like to sleep at your school. He said he reads a lot. He takes French, German and Latin besides his scientist subjects. For our eighth birthday, it was *A Sunday on La Grand Jatte* by Georges Seurat, signed Joyeux anniversaire, Le Fred.

When we turned nine, he sent from *Four Tulips: Grote Geplumaceerde (The Great Plumed One), and Voorwint (With the Wind) (detail)* by Jakob Marrel, and I had to look up what he wrote in a German dictionary: Alles Gute zum Geburtstag! Friedrich.

This year, for birthday number ten, he wrote calligraphy in peacock blue ink and sent Giovanni di Paolo, *Paradise*, with the note, Felicem diem natalem, Fredum, MCMXC.

Because Freddy zips through school grades ahead of everyone else, Mom says he will go to finishing school in a few years before he goes to university. Finishing school is where you learn riding, diving, skiing, sailing and dancing. I think that might be tricky for Freddy, but he'll figure it out.

Have fun getting finished, I wrote on his card. I made a clump of bare black trees with the sunset behind them that looked like stained glass, in ink and coloured pencils. I wonder if he saves my cards, too.

I get back to drawing, where I feel sunshine and float even though I'm sad. When I'm drawing or thinking about pictures, my feelings fly away. Miss Trepanier told me that about reading but it works with drawing, too. It's probably the same for Charlie and Tom and their sports. When I have to bike down to the park and call them for dinner, they don't hear me at all. I think they're ignoring me, but maybe they really don't hear me. I don't hear them when I'm at my desk. Or if I do, it's like I'm far away, like they're across the field when I call. I have to ring my bike bell to get their attention. They usually sneak up on me and jab me at my desk to get mine.

I'm making a picture of Annie and me and some trees we climb. We've named them. I've put the ones we like from different parks all together on one page. I'm not writing their names because they are our secret. The trees will tell her who they are by the way I draw them. I'm not using colour because the trees aren't happy and, besides, they are just starting leaves. We've only had one spring, one summer, one fall and one winter to play in them. One year, but we played almost every day.

Spring Break started yesterday and today Annie is going and we're not even finished Grade Five. I wish we could go explore the river valley one last time. We find treasures and make gnome houses and Annie always makes me giggle.

Mom pops the warm cookies into a tin and, as soon as they're in there, the buttery dough smell in the kitchen fades. Mom leaves out the extra ones: the sort of burnt ones, too close to the edge of the pan, so they have a sidewall. I'm not sure I can eat any. Besides, before I get down and up from my desk, the boys beeline in and grab the rejects and hurry outside to snarfle them up.

Mom wants to see my drawing. She knows who the people are, but she doesn't know about the trees.

That's Sunnyside. That's Swinger, this is Spyer and that one's Picnic.

The names bubble out of me, but it doesn't really count because Mom doesn't know they are secret and, anyway, Annie is going.

Mom says, what about that first day, when the two of you ran to the corner park to find pussy willows?

I draw in a few fuzzy bushes in *Forest of Friends*. When we came back that day, the moms were drinking tea and giggling. Mom remembers, because she's taking a big breath. I take one, too.

Don't forget to sign it, she says.

So in the corner I put, For Annie, and in the pussy willows but kind of hidden like artists do, my name. And two pine cones on the forest floor. For when we played squirrels.

Wait, says Mom, when I finish.

She takes the drawing and goes in Dad's office and uses his super-duper desk photocopier. The kids aren't allowed to use this machine, and when we have to photocopy a home-work sheet from a friend, or our birth certificate for soccer, only Dad or Mom can do it. Mom has never photocopied my art before, so I'm curious. It's a line drawing, with no shad-ing, so the copy looks printed like a poster. The lines are the same thickness. The erase marks don't show. It makes it look finished, like Mom's drawings at Babci's house. But mine looks like it's from a book that's fresh and new. It doesn't feel like it's mine, without my smudges. It could be from outer space, like the Christmas cards the school made from my Christmas tree drawing one year. They made boxes and boxes of them and sold them to all the families at school. But the picture didn't look like mine anymore. It looked like an illustrator did it. I wonder if we have any more of them, because that card was the first art I've published and I want to send one in the mail to Babci.

I'll find one for her, Mom says. You'll have to keep it safe until Christmas. And this, she holds up the photocopy, is for you.

She puts the date, 1991, lightly, in pencil on the back.

I think of a better title for the drawing, a word I invent-ed with Annie about our trees: *rememory*. I write it quickly on the back of the photocopy, near the date, but I don't write anything on the original. Annie will know. We know what the other is thinking.

When we say goodbye, Annie and Ben and their mom are piled with stuff in the Jalopy, Granny's old black truck. I hand in the cookie tin and my rolled-up drawing tied with blue sat-in ribbon through Annie's window in the back seat. Annie's waving and the baby's screaming, so she gives him the paper roll to hold. He sucks on the edge and bam-bams it on his car seat. Annie shakes the cookie tin. Then she takes out a cookie and breaks it. She does a distraction exchange like I used to do with Stella and gives him half a cookie in each hand. She takes my rolled-up drawing and flaps it out the window. In the wind, the ribbon comes undone, flying from the car as it drives away. I run to pluck it out of a puddle and pitch it and, for a second, it ripples like a kite in the soft, thawed air.

BABY TREE

I SQUISH CLAY ON the wobbly wood-topped table at the community hall, the wet earthy smell of the clay mixing with the smell of peeling varnish and newspaper. The cool clay gradually warms and softens in my sweaty hands. The teacher is Marjorie. She's telling us to get to know our clay. She says it's alive. We're going to make snakes and then coil them into a bowl for clay fruit. I'm going to have a banana, a pear and an orange. I'll make the texture of the orange with a fork. We even get to glaze the clay, but Marjorie cautions that we won't get realistic colours. We're supposed to focus on form, on the shape of the bowl and the fruit.

After class today, Marjorie asked me to babysit her little Nicki so she and her other children can go shopping. Marjorie has five kids and counting, Mom says. I like to go to Marjorie's because she has so many clay pieces and stone sculptures. Her husband travels up North for his university research and brings her carvings of bears and walrus and owls. They're deep green or black or white and all really big and heavy, so even little Energizer Bunny Nicki can't pull them down. I like to touch them with Nicki, feel the smooth cool stone. Daddy brought me a little black bear, a bear cub, for my birthday the last time he went north to Norman Wells. My clay fruit bowl will be like my little bear when it's fired, smooth and solid. And even if, like Marjorie warns, the fruit and the container both look brown in the end, the making of it is mine.

You can't take your eyes off Nicki, ever, says Mom. Marjorie knows I'm home the whole time, so you can phone if you have trouble.

Nicki is a monkey, and crawls up to the windowsills, on top of her highchair, up the bookshelves.

Charlie and Tom were exactly like her, Mom says. Especially when there were two of them. That's why I was so relieved when you sat with your crayons and glue and scissors, hours on end. I could have a whole cup of tea. Watching you fill page after page.

But I'll be following Nicki on her special paths, past the fenced-off basement stairs, and the double-locked outside doors. Marjorie has toys all over the house like she's trying to slow Nicki down, to get her to stop and look at stuff. Like Stella. Even when we're trying to go somewhere, we usually have to wait for Stella. Mom says inspecting and observing are Stella's passion, just like my art and the boys' sports. Stella can spend an hour feeding a leaf to a bug. But Nicki's only interested in what's around the corner, across the room, up there, now that way, then this. We play chase. She squeals when I follow her, and I don't even have to move. I only have to pretend, with a growly smiley face like a friendly bear, and take one baby step.

Nicki clears her path of toys as she crawls. She doesn't go on top of stuff. Instead, she swooshes it out of the way. I can't gather the plastic rainbow doughnuts that stack or the blocks that sort by colour or shape, or I'll lose track of Nicki. I think she's going to run marathons like Auntie Magda's new boyfriend or climb mountains when she grows up. Marjorie thinks Nicki will join Cirque du Soleil.

I have to defrost a green cube and an amber cube of home-made baby food from the ice tray, and mix it with hot water and Pabulum. It looks like vomit but smells like pumpkin. When it's warm, I have to spoon it into Nicki, but I can't get her to stop moving. If I pick her up, she cries. So we make it a game. I take her bowl across the room, and get her to crawl fast to me and take a spoonful, like Auntie Magda's boy-friend takes a sip of purple Gatorade from her at a running race. Then I get her to chase me across the other way, spoon in another mouthful, back and forth. She loves it. When her mush is gone, I make her an obstacle course out of propped up couch cushions. She belly laughs when she figures out how to knock them down and go over them instead of going around them.

I try to get Nicki to draw. She has chubby felts. When I uncap one for her, she has to smell it first. She gets more on her face than on the page. But when I make a fast drawing of her on a cardboard box for her toys, she stops long enough to take my felt pen from me and move it on the paper. I chuckle because she makes a circle person with eyes and stick legs.

It's a *dobie*, my name for the circle people I used to draw when I was little. Mom still has some of them taped up in the laundry room. I show Nicki how to put in stick arms and a smile.

My portrait of her is in many colours because she wants each pen I'm using, and so I give them to her one by one to keep her interested. She makes little swirls in different colours around her big dobie. To me, it looks like Nicki whirling on a merry-go-round. Even though her body isn't moving, the circles on the page are. When she's tired of the felts, I lift her up and get her to help me tape her art to the fridge and then

I pretend to be the merry-go-round. I spin her gently around in the kitchen. Then we clean up the couch cushions so I can spin her faster and faster in the living room, dropping her head lower, then upside down. She squeals, thrilled.

And in a swirling spray of amber-green, all over me, the carpet and up the shelves so even the walrus and the polar bears have speckles on them, Nicki spews out her lunch. She's choking, struggling to breathe. I pat her back, and lay her on one arm, head down, like with the doll in my babysitting course. Nicki's turning red and sputtering and her little body squirms so I can hardly keep hold of her, and I sort of drop her. She startles, lets out one big cough and more puke, then cries. Really loud.

Oh, Nicki, are you okay? I'm sorry! Oh, Nicki!

Her eyes are mad blue and she spreads goo all over her face. I hug her anyway, mess and all. I'm crying, and she's crying. She's sad, and she's mad, but she's breathing and rubbing the awful mush into her eyes. She keeps wailing until I take her to the bathroom and start the tub. She loves baths more than anything. I take off my sweatshirt and hold Nicki tight while we clean up the mess in the living room with my shirt, even the splotches on the carvings, with the sleeve, and stuff it in a plastic bag.

Nicki splashes in the tub. She won't let me use a washcloth on her face, so I get her on her tummy, legs kicking and wash the throw-up off with my hand. Then I put her on her back and give her a shampoo, which she doesn't like at all. She screams at me again because she gets shampoo in her eyes. I use a towel to wipe it away. Then I sit her up and hold each of her hands in mine and try clapping together: Toshie-toshie tosh-ie, pojedziem do Babci. Nicki calms down when I put her name in, we will go see Nicki, for the second part. She only recognizes the word Nicki in the line of Polish. When we get to her name, we make a big splash.

I keep Nicki in the bath, adding water to keep it warm, because she's happy with her bath toys and I want her stomach to settle and I'm really glad to be sitting in one spot. When I hear Marjorie and the kids, I bundle Nicki up and dry her off and dress her in blue kangaroo sleepers with ears on the hoodie. I wrap her up snug with three corners of her blanket and take her in to Marjorie, who says I can go after I tidy up the bathroom.

My wet T-shirt smells like pumpkin vomit, so I want to get home and get it off. I call out bye to the kids snacking on cut up green apples and pear and banana. The same fruit as in my clay basket, and I get excited about how it will turn out after firing at Marjorie's class next week.

I look at my sketch of Nicki on the box while I'm putting on my coat. It's a fast drawing, but it's Nicki crawling away and turning back, her face asking you to chase her. It makes me grin. Then I pocket my money on the kitchen counter and grab the plastic bag with my dirty sweatshirt by the back door. I walk through fat tumbling snowflakes to the alley and consider throwing my sweatshirt in the garbage, but it's got a puppy print on it. Stella will want it as long as Mom can get the stain out.

I take a deep breath of cold air.

The picture in my mind waiting to be drawn is Marjorie, hands still wet from washing and cutting up fruit, taking Nicki back in her arms like she has never seen that baby before. Even though I'm telling her about the afternoon and Marjorie's giving me instructions, her eyes beam, taking in Nicki's curly damp head, her rosy cheeks, her muscle-body heaviness and drowsy blue eyes all at once. I recognize that look. I've seen it on Mom's face, with Stella. With me, and the boys, even. I've felt it, too. With my Nicki sketch. And my lopsided coil clay fruit basket. It's the look you give your creation.

TREE OF HEAVEN

AUNTIE MAGDA PICKS ME UP in her sleek white convertible with the top down. She wears a tangerine scarf and huge sunglasses and, even in the breeze, she smells like honey. Her straw swim bag has orange and yellow straw flowers woven in.

I brought lunch, she says. Pickled eggs and cheese and peaches.

We're at the Mill Creek outdoor pool in the ravine, Auntie Magda and me. I have a new two-piece bathing suit that she bought me last week.

You're almost twelve so it's time to get a bikini, she said.

It's pale yellow mesh. Auntie Magda says it will show off my tan, but I'm white as paper. It's been raining all June. I think it looks okay, but I'm not sure. I hope the top doesn't fall off when I dive. It's a little loose.

Not for long, Auntie Magda says.

Auntie Magda has an orange paisley bikini. It's got gold accents and she wears three gold chains of different lengths around her neck and dangly golden hoops. She has tangerine lipstick to match and her sunglasses have gold lacy rims.

She's reading *A Tree Grows in Brooklyn*. She's skimming it, skipping over batches of pages at once.

What kind of tree is it?

Tree of Heaven, she says. It's really big.

Never heard of it. I study the picture on the front while she flips through pages in the middle, stopping near the end.

From the edge of the pool I can see her eyes behind her sunglasses scan the people even though her head is slightly tilted toward the book. It's starting to get crowded.

Books and houses are very personal, she says. I never show a property to people who don't suit it.

Well, I like trees.

That's why I'm previewing this book. It's for you.

Meanwhile, I swim and dive, and play around with a flutter board. The pool is full of kids my age, and Auntie Magda only goes in to get wet and get out again. Then, she air-dries by taking a few turns walking around the pool, often chatting with people on her way. Then, more Baby Oil. She prefers sunbathing to swimming, she says. She always has a tan, because each winter she goes to Hawaii.

She's talking to the lifeguard. A whistle shines on his bare chest, tanned even darker than Auntie Magda. She's got a movie-star laugh that sounds like there's trickling water in it. His is loud, like a barking sea lion.

For people to trust you to find the absolutely perfect house for them, you need to show you have very good taste, she says.

I know what I like, the guy says. Is that very good taste?

He laughs way too much. I can't stretch out on my towel beside Auntie Magda because the lifeguard guy is still there, so I sit on the edge of the pool, dangling my legs, watching the little kids, since the lifeguard isn't.

A blonde boy, browned like he spends all his time at the pool, asks me to play water ball with him. I glance back at Auntie Magda.

Go on, she says.

The lifeguard stays where he is.

The boy and I toss the orange ball back and forth in the deep end, treading water. It's hard work, but fun. I lose the ball and have to dive for it, and when I come up, he blinks at me.

Woah! He points.

My top is down on one side, the strap trailing down my arm. I duck back in the water, grab the strap and get out of the pool. I let the ball trail into the shallow end so the boy will go get it and I can escape and drip all over the lifeguard, who finally gets back up his highchair while Auntie Magda does both my straps up tight again with a double knot.

Don't worry, Cassie. It's nothing.

But he saw!

He saw hardly nothing. And his eyes were full of water.

My eyes are stinging with chlorine tears. But Auntie Magda, I whine.

You'll be different tomorrow anyway. You're growing every day. The real you is still in progress. He saw maybe a sketch. Not the real you. No one has, and no one will, until you and only you decide. Okay, Cassie?

My face is red from burning up inside and I keep my eyes closed while Auntie Magda rubs Baby Oil on my back and shoulders and legs. I wonder if I'll ever take my clothes off for a boy. I've done it for myself, in private, to music, for fun, before I put on my nightgown. But I won't even take a shower at the pool. I'd rather go home in a wet bathing suit. Yet I pull straps off while I'm on my belly, like Auntie Magda, for tanning.

After a while, I feel pink. Auntie Magda goes to get drinks at the counter. I have my face turned to keep an eye on her bag. When she walks, she does it like everyone is watching the most bronzed and beautiful lady there, and they are. She has a ballerina walk in her bare feet, showing off every muscle in her legs as she goes, as tall as possible, with spiral strands bouncing out of her curly ponytail. There's a little blue star tattoo on her ankle, a golden toe ring and delicate blond streaks in her hair. And in her belly button, a real diamond.

She's gone a while. Now she's having a conversation with a couple and their three children as if she's known them forever. I can hear the pitches of Polish.

I once asked Auntie Magda why she speaks Polish and Mom doesn't.

I have a lot of clients in the Polish community. So it's part of my work to keep it. But your Mom still understands it, you know.

I pull up my bikini straps, flip over, pick up her book and get hooked.

I thought you'd like it, Auntie Magda says when she gets back with our ice-cold Diet Pepsis.

I like that in this book Francie has a tree that listens to her, and watches her, and becomes her friend. I understand this girl, even though she lives in New York and I live in a city far away in Canada. She reminds me of my friend Annie who moved to Vulcan, which feels as far away as New York. I tuck myself into some shade under a red pool umbrella, pretending that it's a Tree of Heaven, and read until the water ball boy packs up to go. He sneaks a look over to me but I keep my eyes in my book. I get Auntie Magda to check my bikini top again.

Sweetie, your straps won't slip off when you're a little more filled out.

I don't know about that. She's extremely filled out, and the clasp holding her top together in the front looks like it will burst, especially when she bends over to stretch out her lower back in a yoga pose.

Because she's always on the road, Auntie Magda's car is her office, and she needs to work out her driving muscles. She does yoga every morning and every evening, on a purple mat, with cushions and a palm tree and tall fragrant candles on purple glass dishes. I sniff them on each visit: lavender, eucalyptus and cedar. Auntie Magda has her meditation space and Babci has her altar, but Babci's candles are in pickle jars. I wonder if they know how alike they are, daughter and mother, each needing their own little bit of heaven. Maybe I'm the same, with my floating, not only in the pool, but when I draw.

The lifeguard guy squats down to Auntie Magda with two chocolate ice cream cones, so I get out of the pool and back to my towel. He bought one for himself and one for Auntie Magda, and I think he was counting on the length of time it takes to eat one to chat her up some more, but when I show up, he has to give me one of the cones. Score. Auntie Magda takes one lick while he's talking to us, and then he gets called away by some rowdy kids at the diving board. Auntie Magda passes her cone to me. Double score. I eat two-handed and expertly keep chocolate from dripping on my yellow bikini. Auntie Magda sticks to her own food, also like Babci, except she loves Diet Pepsi. She says it has no calories and it peps her up. She buys me potato chips because I ask for them, but she won't even taste one when I offer to share.

No, no. I have to keep my figure.

Keep your waist, I say, and we laugh because it's what Babci says.

Auntie Magda bites delicately into her pickled egg. Her nails are long and they are apricot against the whiteness, but lighter than her fingers.

I like these because I can eat them when I'm driving and they fill me up and don't make a mess, she says.

I drip on the concrete a bit and I must have a little chocolate on my face because out come Auntie Magda's Kleenex. She always has them, in a shiny red satin folding case Babci made her, because Auntie Magda is a crier. I've seen her break into tears at every movie we've watched together, even *The Wizard of Oz* and *E.T.* or *Beauty and the Beast*. I hear her sobbing on the phone when she calls Mom after every boyfriend breakup and she sometimes even cries when she laughs.

What's his name, I ask about Lifeguard Guy, because his eyes rest on Auntie Magda at regular intervals.

I didn't ask, she says, sending him a flirty glance. He's much too young for me. But I gave him my card anyway. You never know, he may have a friend who needs to sell a house. Or buy one. In my work, I need to meet people.

Even at the pool?

Especially at the pool. When I take a day off, like today, I build my contacts. Everywhere I go—shopping, to the gym or the hairdresser. Everyone needs a place to live, so everyone needs a good realtor.

But I think Auntie Magda talks to everybody because, actually, her hobby is boyfriends. Mom listens to Auntie Magda on the phone a lot, but when she hangs up, she shakes her head and sighs. Even Charlie and Tom adore Auntie Magda, and their buddies seriously ogle her. She brings Charlie and Tom sports magazines and posters of their favourite players, and once she and a date even took them out to an Oilers hockey game, with expensive tickets given to her by a client. The boys still talk about the points Gretzky made that night, and how hoarse they got from screaming and that was four years ago, just before he got traded. Last time Auntie Magda came over, she let the boys take turns driving her around the block in her white convertible. She calls it Baby.

When it's time to go home, I'm stiff from reading and burnt, back and front, even though I put my T-shirt on over my bathing suit a while ago. In her pool bag, Auntie Magda carefully packs her mini transistor radio, her Baby Oil in its own little plastic bag with a pink twist tie, her snack containers, her cigarettes, her golden lighter, her business card case and her towel. She wears a white sheer cover-up that shows her tan right through. Her lipstick is still perfect because she only drinks out of a straw. She slides her terra cotta toes into her flowery sandals in the change room and out we go to the hot parking lot.

Baby, she croons. Like it really is one.

We get in the sun-heated seats, and I'm glad for the warmth because I'm a little chilly from my damp suit under my shorts on the windy drive home. I shiver, once, and at the next red light Auntie Magda drapes her towel, which is still dry, over me. When Auntie Magda drops me off she says bye, my dear, and wait, I need to inscribe your book. She takes out Dziadziu's black fountain pen, the one she says is lucky for her real estate deals, and slowly, elaborately, writes loose left-leaning letters on the front page: With much love from Auntie Magda, July 22, 1992, a heavenly day together.

Buzi, buzi, she says, reaching out to me.

So I give her little kisses like she does, both cheeks, buzi, buzi. Her warm honey scent still lingers near her neck.

I want to go in and change and get some aloe gel for my back and read for the rest of the day and night. I thank Auntie Magda again for the book and the swim and the lunch and the bikini, even though I hope I'll be too big for it next time and never wear it again.

FAMILY TREE

I AM NOT AN OCTOPUS! Mom yells.

Everyone shuts their mouths, as if she might sweep out her tentacles and smack us with her suction-cups. The boys need their lunches double-large because otherwise they'll eat it all after morning practice, I need a permission form for my Grade Seven field trip to Drumheller, Dad needs a signature on a paper for the bank and Stella needs her zipper fixed and a Kleenex and a hug. Mom's got the plastic mustard bottle ready to squirt us all with yellow octopus ink.

Instead, in the moment of quiet, she gets us all what we need, and we hurry out the door, to school, to work, to play. Mom has the dishwasher, the morning's breakfast dishes, lunch makings, school letters, game schedules and newspapers in a jumble about her. I take a last look before I leave. Her arms are moving so fast that it seems like she has more than two. If I blink, I imagine at least five or maybe an octopus eight, at full speed. I smile inside, but it creeps outside, and Mom grins back at me.

See you later alligator, she says.

I keep thinking about octopi. I wonder how they manage all their arms. I try to figure out how one arm would know what the other seven are doing. There must be a built-in brain in each tentacle that sends messages to the other ones, so they don't all end up doing the same thing or all forgetting to do the same thing. And what if they lose one? I know that a starfish can re-grow arms, but what about an octopus? I look it up during library time: if an octopus arm is cut off, it grows back! It's called regeneration.

After school, it's sunny, but I don't want to hear the plunk-plunk of the boys playing basketball on the driveway or the little-girl opera of Stella making food out of sticks and pine-cones and sand. I go where I always go after a long loud day at school. At my art table, I'm in my cloud, safe from sound except Mom cooking supper, listening to French CBC. French talking on the radio sounds like music to me because it's so fast and I only understand a word here and there. Mom listens to keep up her French. She says once you know one other language, it's easier to learn the next one.

I'm working on another tree. This one is in a British Columbia forest, where we went last summer on holidays. Stella and I felt like we found the enchanted forest because of the moss on the ground and lichen dripping from the trees. There were so many colours of green, all so glossy and wet, that even on a sunny day it was dark and mysterious. We made a fairy garden from sticks and rocks and moss. I'm doing a watercolour trying to get that moist look on the trees from misty rain. I want to show the hush in the enchanted forest, the feeling that magic can happen there.

There's a wail from the driveway. Not the usual whooping of the boys when they score, but the scream for Mom that says they're going to the hospital. Mom turns down the stove, grabs her purse and quilting bag and leaves me in charge. When I yell that I don't know what to do, she runs out with her arms up, her way of saying, wing it! Then she rushes off to the van with the bleeding boy and sends the unhurt one inside.

He fell, says Tom. But he wouldn't let go of the ball, so he fell on his arm. Tom slaps his right arm below the elbow.

My gut shivers. Poor Charlie.

Probably busted it, says Tom.

Tom says it like it happens everyday, but it's not his fault and not his turn, so no big deal. It's way worse when the boys get into fights. They turn into snotty screaming monsters, wrestling each other in the leaves, rolling and flailing, bruising and beating up the one person in the world they can't stand to be without. Even Louis tries to break them up, barking until they stop.

Tom hoists his knapsack on one shoulder and Charlie's on the other and takes a box of cereal and a half-full double carton of milk upstairs. When one brother is at the hospital, the other one does homework. Like a prayer.

In my forest, I paint in a second tree that has fallen beside the first one. It balances the standing tree, and makes it less lonely, even though the second tree is broken at the bottom of the trunk. The broken trunk will grow new branches because trees, like octopi, regenerate.

But supper waits, half-made, and Stella hiccups from hunger. So we get busy. Stella sets the table. She drops a glass, which breaks in two clean pieces, but she wipes the area with a damp paper towel so Louis won't hurt a paw on a tiny shard. I check all the pots and turn the rice right off like Mom does to steam it. I taste the sweet and sour ribs, add a plop of hot sauce and stir everything to make sure nothing is burning. I make the salad and we dress up the table with flowers and napkins. Stella insists on making name cards. I get a ladybug on mine. Mom gets a spider (Stella's favourite). Tom gets a black beetle, Stella gives herself an ant (the queen, of course) and Dad gets a bee. Charlie has a pupa because he's at the hospital.

By the time Dad gets home, he's talked to Mom, who quilts during the wait with Charlie. He's had an X-ray and is in the casting room. It calms her to stitch, especially when the boys are getting stitches, but also at music lessons and soccer practices and basketball games and even movies. I'm the same, with my sketchbook. Her hands, like mine, like to be making.

The four of us eat dinner, quietly. I try to get Dad to guess my secret ingredient, but he eats too quickly and drinks a lot of water. Tom, who eats at wild-animal speed, catches a ride to the soccer field with Dad, who's going straight to the hospital to trade places with Mom. Which leaves me with Stella the picky eater, Louis begging for any scraps and dishes to load. I turn French CBC back on. I pick out a few words: bonne nuit, la lune, chez la maison.

Mom arrives home, famished, to find the kitchen only partly cleaned up. I left the food out for her. I didn't do the counters yet because Babci phoned, and I had to tell her the whole story of Charlie. Mom scrubs out the sink. She eats while she wipes counters and reorganizes the fridge.

I drift back to my art table and my watercolour. I don't like the way it has dried, but I try a few more layers of colour and the tree trunks get more solid and the branches are less wispy, so I decide it's after the rain instead of in the rain.

Whatever magic that was there has already happened. You can tell I got interrupted. I'll have to start again.

Mom makes plates for Charlie and Tom, who always eat again when the wounded one comes home. She works up to her usual octopus speed. Then she pauses.

Your arms took over for mine.

Stella, too. That makes four arms, Mom.

Your brothers' would make eight.

She holds one arm in the other as if it was Charlie's broken one, willing it to regenerate.

Octopus Mom. She has two arms for each of us.

LEMON TREE

THE PAINT CHIP SAYS Dusk Sunflower but it reminds me of the heart-shaped golden leaves on the whispering aspens in fall. The wall colour I've picked out by myself and painted with Dad turned out pretty intense. It's darker than I thought it would be. Mom suggested that we buy a shade or two lighter, but I'll grow into it. In summer, maybe it will be less shocking when there's more sun in here.

I finally have my very own bedroom and an art space all my own. Dad put a lock on the door, too. I've moved my art supplies from the sunroom into built-in bookshelves beside a real drafting table from a friend of Dad's, an architect. We made one wall half in cork to tack up two-dimensionals. Spread above my art table, under the window, we installed a long inspiration shelf for three-dimensionals: coloured glass, rocks, feathers, buttons, shells, pinecones, keys, balls, spools and my animals from Dad, the stone bear and a new one, a bird carved from bone. I rearrange this shelf often. Some days I put it in colour order, and some days from light to dark. Also textural order, smooth to rough. To make my ideas pop, some days I add random bits I find in my jacket pockets or I clear everything away to focus on one object.

Dad moved his study to the basement, so Stella could have his old office upstairs for her bedroom. He painted it a serene Eau de Nil Green even though Stella's as laid-back as her lizard. She also has jars of live insects and a small aquarium. Mom didn't let her have rodents when we shared a bedroom, but now there's a gerbil. Stella has to keep her door closed, like the boys, because of the smell, but she won't open her window in case it gives her creatures a cold.

The boys still have their room together because one wouldn't know what to do without the other. Now that they're teenagers, they look more and more alike. Lots of people mistake them for twins even though they're a year apart: same dark hair, braces, fast moves and long legs. Tom tries to be taller than Charlie, faster than Charlie, tougher than Charlie, hairier than Charlie. They didn't want anything changed in their room when we renovated, but Mom got them new sheets anyway, and she finished their matching quilts. I never go into their musty mess. And now that I've got a lock, they won't be coming in here ever again.

The boys got into big trouble. They were in charge while Mom and Dad were out. They found my sketchbook in the kitchen, the new one from Auntie Magda that's bound in real red leather, and used it to write game plays with their horrible Grade Twelve hockey friends, and then tore their pages out. I heard them and got it back, but then they got into Dad's whiskey and Mom's wine. Charlie and Tom had to buy new whiskey for Dad, sherry for Mom and a sketchbook for me.

They give me a pink Barbie sketchbook. I throw it in the garbage.

Since when do you not like Barbie?

Tom, when was the last time I played Barbies?

Besides, my Barbie outfits aren't schlocky like the ones you buy. Mine are haute couture by Babci. They could be in a museum someday. They don't look anything like the pink sparkly workout Barbie on the cover of that sketchbook.

Charlie pulls the Barbie book out of the garbage. He holds it out.

Come on, Cassie, we just used a bit of your paper.

It's for my art and it's private!

We thought you'd like this one.

I don't say anything so he chucks it back in. I don't say anything to either of the boys for a week, I'm so mad. They also get yard work, and I get a holiday at Babci's, alone. Before I go, though, I rake through the garbage for the Barbie sketchbook and shove it under my bed. To remind me how mad I am.

Today Mom's got a lost look, like the stick trees outside. All the leaves have fallen, and the trees look chilled, like they can hardly wait for snow to cover them up. She calls me down from my new room to move the playhouse. I haven't been in it since way before I could fit in the door. I never liked the playhouse because it was dark inside. Stella doesn't like being indoors anywhere. She prefers the wind and everything that flies in it.

I'll put my gardening stuff in here, says Mom.

Dad made it. He keeps a photo in his office of the day he finished it, the one and only time us four kids were in the playhouse together, poking our heads out its two little windows. The boys were already twelve and eleven.

Mom and I get Charlie and Tom and Stella and we all lift and slide and plunk the playhouse down on the gravel in the side yard. Mom's cleared it and raked the gravel level. Louis sniffs and gets in the way. The playhouse now leaves him less space for his doggie business.

But it's more private than before, says Stella to Louis. You'll like it.

Louis gazes at her with adoration. He trusts Stella completely.

Annie and I were going to have a sleepover in the playhouse, but we never did. I've sent her two birthday cards. I wonder if she's moved again, and I'm happy if she has, because I only got one note from Vulcan, Alberta: Vulcan is dead. I keep sending her cards anyway because I like making cards. Mom does the addresses and stamps. I saw her photographing one before she put it in the envelope. She photographs quilts she gives away, too.

In the backyard, a big bald patch stares up at us. Without the playhouse, the yard looks like a spaceship lifted off and killed a square of grass. Stella stirs and pokes and oohs in the blank spot. Bugs awaken in the cold, and scramble for cover. There are centipedes and beetles, spiders and worms. I bend down with Stella to watch and some muddy yellow pokes out of bleached weeds. It's a ball, a small bouncy ball from a birthday party loot bag three years ago. From Annie. She gave me the yellow one especially, because it was the same colour as Babci's apples, and Annie loved them. I snatch up the ball and hope Annie has an apple tree in Vulcan. I'll put one on my next card for her.

The day I get my holiday away from my brothers and they get to rake and bag leaves, I get a princess lunch alone: fluffy white sesame bread, cold sausage, horseradish mustard and garlic pickles. After, Babci sends me to the basement for a box of apples to take next door. Mrs. Sekula has an apple tree, but it doesn't make apples anymore, so she envies Babci's, which overflows with tangy yellows, perfect for szarlotka cake, every year.

Mrs. Sekula's tree forgets, Babci says.

Ever since Mrs. Sekula's husband died and her two daughters married and moved away and never visit, her apple tree has not bloomed. Babci told Mrs. Sekula to get rid of her bitterness and maybe the tree will remember to fruit again.

I bite away my own still-burning bitterness at my brothers by chomping on another pickle, which fizzes like 7-Up. When I take the apples next door, Mrs. Sekula's not home so I leave the box on her back steps. Hanging from her tree, there's a plastic lemon tied on with a strip of raggedy fabric.

Babci used strips of ripped white cotton once and only once to twist my hair into ringlets. I had to sleep overnight with bulges of tight rolled fabric at my scalp. When I complained the next morning, she said, sometimes you suffer. Then she combed each ringlet carefully around her finger into a sausage, and tied a yellow satin bow on the top of my head, to go to her church bazaar. I let her do it for the bazaar, for the delicate egg and pickle sandwiches with their crusts cut off on paper doilies, the fancy tea cups, the plants and knickknacks for sale, the pretty Polish ladies. With my own money, I buy a white crocheted doily, its complex lacy windmill pattern transfixing, to me. Babci doesn't like them. Too fussy, she says. But I'll tack it to my bedroom wall, and let the gold shine through.

Every time I visit Babci's after that, I check on Mrs. Sekula's tree. Every time, there's another lemon. Sometimes, a lime. Babci laughs, and gives me a plastic lemon, not quite empty, from her fridge. I suck on the last of it for the thrill of straight lemon juice and, without being seen, toss it under Mrs. Sekula's tree. The next day, it is neatly tied on. I keep count over the winter. I wonder if this is a Ukrainian Christmas tradition, to decorate an outside tree with lemon "balls." I save a lemon and a lime from home, too, and leave them on the falling down fence for Mrs. Sekula the next time. I even get Mom to buy a few extra lemons and squeeze them into a jar so I can take another one of each to Mrs. Sekula the time after that. They stick out, yellow and green in the snowy yard. By spring, I count seven lemons and three limes.

On Mother's Day, Babci asks Stella to set the table and sends me to the garden to collect fresh chives for the sour cream. Mrs. Sekula sits on a wooden kitchen chair with its back broken off. She gets up and calls me over to the fence, speed-talking in Ukrainian, but I don't need to understand her words: her tree is full of blossoms. The lemons and limes still hang here and there, in the froth. She points to the bees, in love with her tree, and I nod and grin. She claps her hands and smiles so wide she loses her wrinkles. I try to reach one of the lemons to take it down but she stops me, tears in her eyes. She wants to leave them. And I understand. The lemons and limes remind her how much she wanted the apples, and they make the apple blossoms somehow holy. She's sacrificed her own bitterness like empty limes and lemons. Instead of hiding them, she shows them, to let it go.

When I get home, I take out the Barbie sketchbook from under my bed, wipe away the dust bunnies and draw Mrs. Sekula's tree. I make a flipbook, like Freddy showed me once way back in kindergarten: it makes a movie, Cassie, try it. It starts with the bare, sad tree, then gets one lemon, and then more, and limes, until the blossoms start, and fall, and then the green apples that turn to red. I use coloured pencils for the lemons, limes and apples. The tree is in ink, and the blossoms and leaves are outlined only. When it is done, so the Barbies don't show, I glue on a drawing of the first, sad, forgetful tree.

I leave Stella inspecting the bare ground in our backyard and Mom wondering about a patio on the dead stretch of lawn, and take Annie's yellow ball to the sink. The colour of the ball melts to butter as the dirt scrubs away. I carry the ball, small enough to hide in my hand, upstairs to my room and position it on my new shelf. Then, like a puff of fresh air, for one second, long enough to be real, like a warm dreamlight, I feel that Annie is okay. It is magical. I know for sure, but I don't know how. Like letting go of a balloon and watching it float overhead. Like Mrs. Sekula, watching her blossoms fall off in the rain, full of faith that there will be fruit.

In my own yellow room with the door locked and the window open, I have faith, too. It feels like floating, like it always has, but now I have a name for it. Trees have it, so why shouldn't I? I don't know if it's the same as Babci's faith in her bedroom altar, her candles and God, but it is mine.

The tree I'm working on now is one of many elm trees on the neighbourhood boulevards, but this one is a dancing tree. I admire it every day on my walk to junior high. Last year, when the city was doing road construction on that corner, I worried that they'd hurt it or cut it down, but the workers surrounded it with a temporary wooden box to keep it safe. When the box came off I borrowed Mom's camera and took shots from many angles and put the prints on my cork wall. It's the only tree I've ever seen that has a curve like the backbend and waist and hips of a dancing girl, with a sprig of leafy twigs coming out her bottom like a little skirt, and arms reaching up, overhead, embracing the sky.

HOLLOW OAK

CUP-A-NOODLES FOR LUNCH. Groan. That means waiting in the line-up at the Grade Eight microwave. I nibble at my grapes because I've got no one to talk to. Except the Weird Lady. She stands at the microwave in her flimsy plastic gloves, a roll of paper towel under one arm and squirt bottle in the other. She's really short. While you wait, she opens your jacket and reads your T-shirt. Great. Today I'm wearing my SOUL shirt. I zip up my hoodie.

Nobody talks to the Weird Lady. In the hallway, you zoom away in the other direction if she shuffles up in her dirty old raincoat, done up tight, a worn saddlebag across one shoulder. She writes down the words from your T-shirt with a turquoise pom-pom pen in a matching notebook and makes you say them out loud. Then she repeats them. It's pretty weird.

The guys ahead of me ignore her. They're wearing hockey jerseys and she writes down Wayne Gretzky, Mark Messier and the great team they left behind, the Edmonton Oilers. Like she's never heard of them. Like I say, weird.

So she comes up to me. But before she can unzip my hoodie, I use Dad's hockey advice and get on the offence. I ask her a question. It's so loud in the lunchroom I have to bend down to her ear and shout.

What's your name?

Yeva.

Where are you from?

Russia, Germany, Japan and Iran.

Wow. She's like a walking Social class.

I ask, why do you write down everybody's words?

To learn English.

Why T-shirts?

I like kids.

I leaf through her notebook.

Puma.

Reebok.

Ralph Lauren.

But she's fast. She pulls off her plastic glove and unzips my hoodie.

So I explain SOUL. With difficulty.

What's inside you that nobody sees, I say.

Yeva pats her chest, and has a lot of trouble pronouncing it, but I'm patient. My noodles are still warming up.

Me inside, she says.

She's got it. I nod.

The jerk behind me hyena laughs.

Then I read his T-shirt: BREED. I define that one for Yeva.

Rabbits, many babies?

Yeva titters like a bird.

The guy turns red. I'm not sure he's completely clued in.

I can't see any of my friends, so I eat my noodles while reading the notice board, but Yeva follows me there, both gloves off now and points to words in her notebook. I try to explain that Nike and Adidas are brand names. I know from my brothers that Nike is the Greek goddess of victory and Adidas is code for All Day I Dream About Sports.

I get her to take her raincoat off and point to the label, and then she understands. It's Burberry. I've seen this in Babci's *Vogue*. Yeva knows quality, I guess, but just doesn't wash it.

She smiles like I'm her new best friend. I hope not. She makes me circle all the designer names in her notebook.

There's a lot of label love here. This is junior high.

In the hallway, I avoid everyone, because they're mostly taller than me, but I really avoid Yeva, the only one who isn't. The Weird Lady has no boundaries. We learned about it in Health. If you touch someone's T-shirt as they walk past you, you're invading their personal space. Yeva grabs and she has a strong grip. She also goes for wrists, hoods, belts, bags, headphones, anything to make you stop and show her your shirt. She has eyes that dig. Claw hands. And a piercing voice, like a magpie.

What's that say?

Lots of people have stopped wearing T-shirts with words, me included. Who wants to get attacked by a refugee?

But she picks me out of the crowd day after day. She wants a conversation. That's why she's here, to learn the language. I don't think she needs the few dollars a day for being a lunch supervisor until I see her select an unbruised apple and a Mandarin orange, still tucked in its green tissue paper, from the garbage can. Some kids throw out anything not in cellophane, including homemade sandwiches. But Yeva only takes discarded fruit. Mom makes me bring home my apple cores and orange peels in a Ziploc bag for the garden compost, but she also wants evidence that I ate my fruit for the day.

Yeva doesn't have grandchildren at this school. I asked. That's lucky, like that wouldn't be social suicide. Her kids live in far-off places.

Singapore. Yeva says it's the cleanest city in the world.

Miami, Florida. The oranges there are the best.

Inuvik. She's never been. But she's going soon.

Or at least that's what she says. I'm not sure I believe her. I'm pretty sure people who garbage pick also pretend. She has no grandchildren yet. She wants some. She's learning English so she can talk to them when they are born. She doesn't like going to classes because they go too slow. She knows seven languages. I count them on my hands.

Russian is first.
Then German,
French,
Ukrainian,
Japanese,
Persian
and English.

Those last six are from kids at school grounds, at parks, in shopping malls. To test this, I ask her to say, Hello, my name is Yeva, in all seven languages. She does it without even a beat in between each, counting backwards from English by pinching each of my fingers. Creepy, much.

I should have known to watch out for her out of school, too. At Southgate Mall, Sue and Kimmy and I are at the food court when Yeva spies us, yelling, eh, eh, eh! She sits down with us just as we're digging in to our stir-frys. Kimmy and Sue have their mouths full, trying to finish fast. Yeva stares at my chow mein and tells us her life story in one minute.

Bad men kill mother and father. Bad men has axe. House on fire. Sisters run. I climb tree. House burns. Cat climbs tree to me. Sisters no come back. Find nuts, fill pockets. I go to city, to auntie. I sew for auntie. Six years I hide. Cat dies. I go. No tell auntie. Your age, I get job. In factory. I sew. Owner keeps me. Sew all day. Cook and clean at night. Nice house. Nice family. New language. German. Four children. They teach me. Family moves. I find husband. Good man. Three babies. He dies. I sew at home. Smart children. Go to good school. Boy at Inuvik. Cold there. Cold always. You nice. Nice girls. You talk to me.

My friends haven't finished swallowing. They get up. They don't want to be nice. It's been a long winter and they have an agenda.

Come on, Cassie, we need to find shoes!

In a minute.

Hurry up!

Meet you at Payless.

I wave them off.

Yeva is still inside her tree of memory. I fold my paper napkin. I tell her about my Babci, who hid food wrapped in cloth napkins during the war. She was only a child, but she was sent to hide the white bundles in a hollow tree: sugar, butter, flour, tea. Soldiers moved through the woods, but she and her little sister went out to play around the tree and bring back what was needed in big pockets sewn inside their coats.

Yeva nods. My Babci, like Yeva, has been in the woods.

Eat you lunch, Yeva says, and I am lost in the dark forest, too.

I wonder if Babci and Yeva sew away their bad memories. I wonder if that's why they make clothing, which is useful like the pockets that saved their lives. I only make pictures.

Kimmy and Sue are still trying to get my attention, and suddenly I feel the sting of Thirteen Forever, like Freddy signed his last card: John Singer Sargent, *Figure in a Hammock, Florida.* I ignore Kimmy and Sue.

I offer Yeva my stir-fry. I've only managed to eat a few forkfuls. She accepts it, and my unwrapped chopsticks, and expertly eats down to the carton. I sip on my 7-Up. I wonder where she lives. She's got a battered suitcase on wheels that she pulls around with her. It's got tiny stickers stuck on top of more stickers. They're fruit stickers: Ecuador bananas, California oranges, Washington apples. That's how many pieces of fruit from the garbage cans at school?

I wonder if she's homeless. But then she began life alone in a tree.

No, she says, I go. All the time, I go.

Where? I ask.

Inuvik! To my son.

She pulls out her ticket folder and shows me the date. Monday. I've never seen an airline ticket up close before. As Charlie and Tom would say, sexy, wow.

How long will you stay?

Long! Long time.

I wonder if she's been sleeping outside to get used to the cold. In the bus shelter. She probably loads up on fried food first. People in the north eat a lot of fat so they don't feel the cold, Dad says. He gets Kentucky Fried Chicken when he works up in Norman Wells. Mom can't stand the smell of KFC, but Dad takes us kids to the drive-in for car suppers with the windows open, sometimes.

And then?

Then Florida. To my girl, Darah.

I think of Yeva making lines like a net on the map of the world, from north to south and west to east. If you don't live in one place, does that mean the world is your home, a nest with threads from every place you go? And everyone you meet is your friend? Or has a thread that sticks to you?

Good food. Thank you.

It's okay. Glad you like it.

Where go your friends?

I'll find them.

Behind Yeva, Kimmy and Sue wave to get me away. They're laughing. How can they laugh at bad men has axe.... I climb tree?

I wait until Yeva finishes and pull out my sketchbook from my floppy leather hand-me-down bag from Mom. I want to know what kind of tree. She points at the one in my book most like the one she hid in.

Leaves falling down, she says.

I wish I had my tree book from Dad. To identify your trees, from their cones, their bark, their leaves, he said.

I sketch a few shapes of leaves. On a blank page, Yeva traces the curvy in and out lines of the oak leaf with her thumb. I outline her marks with my pencil.

Smells like tea? I ask.

She nods, slowly. Taste bad.

She's tasted them? Mom collects and crushes oak leaves to get rid of slugs.

Bitter, I say.

She asks for the spelling and writes in her own book: bitter makes you cry.

I write in her book: good luck.

She knows that one and draws a shamrock beside it.

I draw a little globe and add Yeva in her raincoat at the top of the world and, because I know from Social class that in Inuvik there aren't any trees at all, I sign my name with a little pine: Your Friend. I need to send a tree with her. To let her know her story has a place to grow.

I leave Yeva in the food court reading the inscription over and over, smoothing over the page in her notebook. I used Babci's Polish name for me, Kasia. Yeva says it like Babci.

Yeva will start a new notebook for Inuktitut.

I'll put her in my oak trees. Y was here, scratched on the trunk, or maybe just a Y in the pattern of the bark, hidden, and a Z, too, for Zofja, my Babci.

Kimmy and Sue pull me into the closest shoe store, the most expensive one.

Do you wanna be weird like her?

Kimmy pounces and protects at the same time, steering me out as soon as the saleswoman asks if she can help us.

She ate your food, Sue says. Is she going to eat ours?

We watch as she packs their stir-frys into one carton and ties it to her rolling suitcase.

Scavenger, Kimmy says.

Gross, says Sue.

She must be hungry, I say. We won't see her again. She's leaving for Inuvik.

Like we believe that.

Yeah.

She showed me her ticket. For tomorrow.

That's a relief, says Kimmy.

Good riddance, says Sue.

I'll never forget her.

But Kimmy and Sue haven't heard me because they are already in the next shoe store. Then I'm with them, and I'm looking at a brown boot on a high shelf. But I'm seeing an oak tree and feeling its trunk in the dark, reaching up and wondering what's in the hollow.

TREE DAY

THE DRAGON ROAR OF a chainsaw fires up. A tree truck is parked outside and three guys with gloves on get ready to change my life. My alarm clock chimes weakly under the screaming growls outside my window. The giant grandmother spruce that I have listened to and loved since I was born is coming down, even though it's green and healthy. If it were mine, I'd strap myself to it. But it's not. It belongs to a lady who lives alone.

I won't have this tree fall on my roof. It's leaning. See? In a big storm, it could kill me, she said to Mom and me over the fence.

We looked up, and then at each other. The tree seemed straight to us.

And, she said, the roots are buckling my brickwork. I could trip and break a hip, and then where would I be?

But we've never seen her use her patio. Talking with her at the fence is rare.

Also, it's clogging my plumbing. Costing me the earth to fix.

It must cost a lot to take it down, Mom says.

Should have done it a long time ago.

As if it's somehow our fault, that she needed a barrier between our yards, but if we weren't there, with all our kids and balls and noise, she would have cut it down sooner. I think she just wants to live longer than the tree. I know the tree better than I know her, and I've lived next door for fourteen years.

They start by trimming off branches, bottom to top. One guy, who looks like he lives in trees, shimmies up. He leans back into the wide leather belt holding him away from the tree, ripcords the chainsaw, slices and drops bountiful, fanned boughs. I'm supposed to be eating my breakfast, but today Shreddies have the texture of bark. I sip my orange juice, thinking how oranges live on trees susceptible to frost. And saws. Then I try an apple slice, and my eyes well up. It's murder.

I'd ask to stay home from school but I'm not sure I can watch. As I pull the gate closed, a squirrel jumps on the guy up the tree. His chainsaw whines as the critter comes in for round two, but the guy cuffs it away again with his elbow. The squirrel bounces onto another branch destined for destruction. I smile. Creatures, unite.

I breathe in the smell of the boughs. They're full of special hormones that make you feel good. I saw that on a nature show. Different trees have different healthy hormones. My tree's parting gift. The next moment, I have to hold my breath. Chainsaw gas pollutes the tree's fragrant sacrifice. It makes me lightheaded. The saw drowns out the chittering of the squirrel.

In class I feel draggy. I keep drawing her, the grandmother tree, in Language Arts. She was there before any of us. Except maybe the woman next door, whose yard will now open wide to our backyard. No more privacy. No more shade. No more birds. I've collected the sticky cones for crafts and wreaths and, before then, play food with Stella, and my cheeks get wet in Math. My teacher excuses me to go to the washroom. Instead, I sneak outside and sob against the red-brown brick wall of the school facing the parking lot. When I stop with a shuddering sigh I still hear the chainsaw squeal, two blocks away.

What's wrong?

It's Darryl, the kid who plays bagpipes. He's never in class. He wanders the halls, doing odd jobs for teachers. Gifted, I've heard Mom say, which sounds like Freddy. Freddy's smart and thoughtful, but I wonder how Darryl is gifted. I've never even heard him talk to another kid before.

My tree is...

Falling down?

Yeah.

What kind is it?

A spruce.

I don't say: it makes these huge long cones; it has a squirrel in it, and birds. Or, trees are sacred. Lives depend on them. I have a forest of them in my sketchbooks.

Darryl listens like he hears me say it all anyway. Then he says, It's a Husqvarna.

He spells it for me.

H-u-s-q-v-a-r-n-a. It's a superior brand of chainsaw.

This kid has pitch.

He guides me away from the school ground without being seen by the office staff. We use the back alleys, then through the corner park and get to my house as the lumberjack guys stop for a coffee break. They actually wear red plaid shirts.

But the tree. She is bare of her branches, a thick naked length of footholds to her crown. A birdhouse, put up by Dad a long time ago, sprawls broken in peeling pieces on our side of the fence. I painted that birdhouse, red and green, when I was in playschool. I try to fit the pieces back together, but they've rotted.

Then Darryl, bagpipe guy, whistles. I've never heard anyone whistle like that. There's a tune, sad, but somehow triumphant. Louis plunks on the patio, head on paws, but eyes and ears alert like Darryl's the Pied Piper. And the lumberjacks, smoking, with one side of their orange ear mufflers hanging down, take both sides off to listen. My mom comes outside. Even the old lady next door stumps out in her housedress to her porch to hear it. A goodbye song for the tree. We all stare at the trunk, tall and alive, yet mostly stripped of green. Darryl is giving her a funeral.

Wish I brought my pipes, Darryl says to the silence when he is done. There is a hush, even from the wind.

That was amazing, I say, in a small voice.

He looks up to the squirrel, now silent, front paws in prayer, high in the tree.

It's how I practice, he says. On the bagpipes, you have to improvise. There are only nine notes.

It didn't sound like only nine.

That's because I embellish.

Do you ever.

I'm going to be in the army as soon as they'll take me.

Why the army?

For the funerals. I specialize in funeral anthems.

That was an army song?

No. That was original. For you. For her. It's called "Tree Day."

Only nine notes. I think about having only nine colours. I couldn't cope. It would be crippling.

The lumberjacks rise from their Thermoses of probably black coffee and molasses, ready for the final operation. The skinny guy climbs up to top off the crown. The squirrel, a witness on the tip of the tree till the last moment, barks desperately. We all duck for cover when the crown falls. It lands bigger on the ground than it appears from below. It's studded with mini-green cones, the new tender growth. I feel a sob thrusting up my throat.

Mom says, I called the school. I told them it's a tree day.

Darryl and I nod.

Darryl, I told them you were helping Cassie.

Everyone knows who Darryl is. I thought he only talks to adults because kids aren't smart enough but also, at school assemblies, he wears kilts.

Now I know why. He plays bagpipes at school assemblies because it's his vocation. Auntie Magda has a vocation, too, but not like the nuns. Auntie Magda wants boyfriends, a new one every so often, but not a husband. She says she'd much rather concentrate on her outfits to go out for dinner than put on an apron and cook meals for someone else. Like her, Darryl's devoted to his vocation, and he wants the look, too: the sergeant stripes, the medals, the hat. He's already got the kilt. And his nine lonely notes.

Darryl would rather play music for the dead than talk to girls or play sports. Stella still plays piano. I was allowed to quit when she started. Stella doesn't mind the long hours practicing. She, like Darryl, likes playing for us, and gives concerts for Louis, who gets a dog cookie after each one. Me, I must be like Auntie Magda, because I make my art for myself.

The men in red saw sections of the tall trunk on the ground. The nimble one up there works quickly. The squirrel chitters on, pissed right off.

Darryl stays right beside me. He doesn't take his eyes off the tree. The climber guy gets closer to the ground, and he signals to us. He doesn't seem concerned that the great hunks of tree fall close to the fence or his coworkers. Then he flies us a

Frisbee. It's a tree cookie, from the middle, the thickest part of the trunk. I pick it up off the grass and smell the hormones up close. One edge is a bit ragged. I can sand it off later. We move to the shade and count the rings.

They're called dendochronology rings, Darryl says.

He gets fifty-nine and I get sixty-one. We're not sure if we're supposed to count the xylem or the phloem.

You should bring it to Science and ask, says Darryl.

I wonder how Darryl even knows what's going on in Science class, because he's never there. Maybe he does school by correspondence, or he's already done the work for the year. Probably the teachers give him special projects.

The workers roll out a red machine on wheels.

It grinds the stump to dust, Darryl says.

Do you go to many tree days?

Actually, I do. I practice my anthems. No one hears, usually, because of the chainsaw, the shredder or the stump grinder.

How does he block out the sound and the sadness? His brain must have special filters.

The soldiers at Darryl's army funerals probably won't be fifty-nine or sixty-one years old like the grandmother tree, but they'll have an original anthem, only for them, improvised by Darryl to sing them out. I run my thumb over the lines of years on my tree cookie and imagine the skin of those people. Their different faces against their army uniforms like different colours of wood against green. When Mom bought Crayola Multicultural crayons, I used them for my trees.

Trees, for me, are like humans. No two exactly the same.

I must have said that out loud, because Darryl comments.

Even in your tree cookie, there is diversity.

What?

Different colours.

More than nine, I say.

And darker in the centre, he says.

Lunchtime, calls Mom.

My lunch is in my locker. I should go.

You can stay. Really, Darryl. We have peanut butter.

Someone said he only eats three foods at lunch: apples, peanut butter and white bread.

I only like Squirrel Crunchy, Darryl says. Not Smooth or Skippy or No-name. No jam, no butter, no margarine, no honey. White bread with no crusts, no bran and definitely no seeds. And only Granny Smith apples.

Oh.

Besides, I better see what's going on at school. Enjoy your tree cookie.

Yeah. Sixty-one rings.

Fifty-nine. Count again. I'll tell the office you'll be back for Science.

And I am.

But I don't bring the tree cookie. I don't sand it, either, because the rips of wood and bark are part of the sacrifice. I prop it on my inspiration shelf, to help me draw her, the grandmother spruce, over and over again.

Darryl's song sticks in my head, and every time he sees me in the halls, he looks down without smiling or saying hi, but whistles the first bit from "Tree Day." And without stopping or looking at him, I always whistle back a few of my own. To make nine notes.

TREE OF ABUNDANCE

I'M DRAWING AT HER dining room table, but gradually I notice Babci running back and forth from her bedroom to the kitchen. She usually spends the whole morning in her sewing room and, if she doesn't, she often calls me to help her in the kitchen. Going on a holiday to Babci's now means go with her on the bus to buy the groceries, carry them in, weed and water the garden, do the vacuuming. Stella and I take turns. But today, Babci leaves me be, gives no orders, so I keep on until the smell of apple cake pulls me down from my drawing. There in the kitchen she's set a tea party for three.

Who's coming?

Oh. Dr. Kowalewski.

Why?

He has something for me.

Mom calls him Babci's boyfriend, but I have never met him. He moved in next door after Mrs. Sekula was scooped up by her daughters and plopped in an old folks' home in Vancouver. The plastic lemons and limes are long gone and her apple tree is dying without Mrs. Sekula's praises, but Dr. Kowalewski would not notice. He is almost blind. He never goes outside. But he listens to music. Sorrowful opera music of a woman wailing in Italian. Babci keeps her sewing room window open so she can hear it every day. There used to be chirpy birdsong outside her window, loud enough to be heard over the stitching of the sewing machine. I wonder if the birds listen to the opera, too, or if they get their singing in early before it starts.

When the doorbell rings, I prance to the door first. Dr. Kowalewski bows slightly. He clutches a bulky parcel, wrapped up in brown paper and string. I wonder what it is.

Hi.

Excuse me. My confusion. I am looking for Zofja.

Babci introduces me as Kasia, moves me aside in a stream of singsong Polish and takes his arm to help him in the door. She hangs his heavy coat on a wooden hanger, smoothing the shoulders and patting it as if she made it herself. Dr. Kowalewski chats back to her in Polish but I listen anyway in case he sometimes uses an English word, like Babci and her ladies do, so I can puzzle out the topic of their talk.

He taps the coffee table with his cane and lays the package there, then takes Babci's arm to the kitchen for yellow apple cake. For a nearly blind man, he barely drops a crumb, but this szarlotka turned out especially moist. Babci uses full-fat sour cream. I make my tea white with milk and sugar, but Dr. Kowalewski drinks his steaming and black. He drops his index finger into his tea and checks its temperature before taking a sip. I have three pieces of cake while he and Babci each have a slim one. They don't talk very much, only short bursts in Polish, and I eat away the rest of the silence.

Then we go back to the living room. They take the scratchy couch and I sit on the floor to better inspect the package between us. To my surprise, Dr. Kowalewski switches to elegant, European English. He fixes his watery eyes on me.

I was horribly ill, he says. My son flies from Don Mills, Ontario. He hires cleaners to scour my house. He personally carries bags and bags of journals, my collected magazines and newspapers to the garbage. I block him from my books with my body! My arms, like wings! Framed sketches, created by my dear Jana, his mother, he pulls off the walls!

You're blind, for God's sake! That's what the only son of mine says.

Worst of all, he deposits my pillow in the garbage! Then he goes away. Me, eighty years old, a blind man, I go to the back alley and find the garbage bags and put my hand in each one to feel, to find my pillow. The sketches are not there, so I am calmed. Perhaps he took them as a present from his mother to his own sons. She would be pleased. Feeling outside each bag, then inside, my hands are my eyes. I don't stop until I find it. Imagine, taking the pillow of an old man from under his head! The new one he brings from the store is too puffy, too high. It makes my neck ache. I was not a good father.

He gestures for me to untie the package.

This pillow my mama makes for me. Since I was five years old I have had this pillow. It is dirty, yes. I have never washed it. Only its cover.

In the war, I am in officer prison camp. The first spring Mama sends me my pillow from home. I am happy to have it, but to my sensitive neck it feels different, like something folded hides inside. I wonder, money? I check along the edge, and pull on a red thread. To be sure, I was not blind then! Out comes a little paper. Ah, a lovenote from Mama, I think. I open carefully and inside I find a small amount of seeds. I don't know what they are, but the next day I search and find behind my barracks a sunny space of dirt one metre square, hidden from guards by the fence. I plant the seeds from Mama. I collect rainwater in an old tin. Every day I water, and that summer I have fresh lettuce, radishes, carrots and five perfect tomatoes from one thin plant. I save seeds for the next summer. Five years I keep that little prison garden. It becomes a garden of hope. Even though I languish, I must water my plants. Every time, I feel loved afterward, for loving them. And tasting the vegetables, sharing with my friends, then we are kings!

Dr. Kowalewski wants Babci to wash and recover the pillow, which is losing feathers. He wants to pay Babci for the job, but she scatters that thought away with chiding Polish. One white feather sprouts out as I unwrap and I catch it like a flag of honour before it touches the floor. I'll tuck it into the rough edge of my grandmother tree cookie. A grandfather feather from far away that survived a whole world war!

Then Dr. Kowalewski, who waves away my help, safely descends the many steps to the front gate and climbs the multiple steep steps to his own door. He bows yet again, in case we are watching him. I call out goodbye to let him know that I am, and he nods.

Babci gets right to work on the pillow. She selects a similar fabric, sturdy unbleached cotton, for the cover, washes it in steaming soapy water to soften and irons it dry. Then she rips the seams of the old pillow, and has me hold the new casing while she dumps the feathers in. We pick up any strays and add them. But not the one I'd picked out of the air after I heard his story. That one is in my pocket, mine. When we check for stragglers inside the old yellowed fabric, we find a piece of white thread hanging by one stitch, dangling a thin paper packet the size of Babci's thumbnail!

Carefully, we pull it away from the seam and unfold it. There are no words written, only an eighth-teaspoon of seeds. We shrill.

Babci sews up the new pillow and washes it by hand now that the feathers are safe inside. I can't help thinking that the white feathers are from the snowy eagle on the Polish coat of arms, white on a red background, like on Auntie Magda's bumper sticker on her latest white convertible. This one's called Baby, too.

The next day, the feathers inside the pillow are dry after sunning all afternoon and hanging above the heater all night. Babci fluffs up the pillow in the dryer for five minutes and rewraps it in tissue and places it in a glossy paper gift bag.

We can hardly wait to visit Dr. Kowalewski. Babci phones him to let him know.

Old man need a little time, she says.

Yesterday, why didn't he speak English right away?

He talk to me private.

Like he's your boyfriend?

She shakes her head, nie, nie. He is sour with his son.

What to do about a son who never calls and when he comes it's only to clear out the house? Like he wants Dr. Kowalewski out of the house. Like he wants the house.

The house is very clean. Very little furniture, only nail holes on the walls, no rugs, no plants, nothing but a leather couch, a table and two chairs and books. There are shelves and shelves of books, in no particular order.

Polish.

French.

German.

English.

Italian.

Dr. Kowalewski delights in his pillow. He smells it, feels the new fabric, which is not as soft as the old one, but clean and fresh. He smooths it over his cheek.

Oh, I will sleep like a little child tonight!

Then Babci explains in Polish about the packet of seeds attached to the white thread. Dr. Kowalewski's blank eyes get glassier.

A red thread and a white thread from the old country, he says. From Mama.

He feels the seeds with his fingers. They are the same, unlike the variety of seeds he found fifty years ago. He doesn't recognize them by size or shape. Neither does Babci.

Babci and I have already loaded a bag of garden tools and hung it on the back fence. We guide Dr. Kowalewski outside, and sit him on a chair I've carried from the kitchen.

Where to plant the special seeds? Babci finds a sunny spot near the house, beside the back porch. She makes us fresh sweet lemonade while I pull weeds, overturn the soil and wet it. I plant three short rows. The new flowerbed sits near enough to the ragtaggle fence that Babci can reach to water it from her side with her hose.

When I am finished, I pass the paper packet to Dr. Kowalewski, and he smells it and refolds it and puts it in his heart pocket. He pats it.

He gets sick that summer, and never does come out to tend his mama's seedlings. Babci keeps them watered and I weed. I prune away dead branches from the apple tree to give more sunshine to the plants. The flowers bloom sweetly to the opera music, white and pink and red and lilac. They look like the fabric flowers on the ribboned headband from the Polish dancing costume Babci made for Auntie Magda when she was little.

Babci only knows the Polish words for flowers, so I search Mom's seed catalogue to find the English name. Scented Stocks.

Good for drying, Babci says.

Dr. Kowalewski's mama had thought of the need for food, but also beauty, when her son waited out the war as a prisoner. And now, blind, he can at least smell the flowers.

We cut some and take them to the old man. He sleeps most of the time now. I'm glad he has his pillow back for all that sleeping. A nurse stays day and night. She only lets Babci take in the flowers and hold them near his nose, and makes me stay at the bedroom doorway. The old man murmurs something I can't hear. Babci takes the bundle of flowers and puts them in his hand. He touches them all over. His eyes do not open. He sucks up the smell of the flowers, like my long lost friend Annie's baby brother Ben in the wind under the apple tree. The little baby and the old man know what to do.

Babci holds Dr. Kowalewski's hand and gently touches his forehead and roots of his hair, the way Mom strokes me when I am sick. She hums a lullaby in Polish, "Lulajze Jezuniu." I've heard it at Christmas before. Mom used to sing "Silent Night" to us year-round, too.

When Babci comes out, she says, he goes to the arms of his mama.

While she speaks to the nurse, I go to the bed. The flowers scatter the floor. I pick them up. His eyes are closed.

Mama, he whispers.

I don't think I should say anything. I hold the flowers near his nose, so he can let the scent of them take him home.

Babci brings a vase of water for the flowers and sets it on his bedside table, and lets me arrange the flowers so none of the colours are bunched up and we leave him, his face smooth, breathing lightly but steadily in sleep.

In the winter, Mom drives Babci and me to Dr. Kowalewski's funeral. On the way we watch some school children walking on top of the crusty snow in their schoolyard at recess. The kids are light enough so they don't plummet through the surface. They have oversized toques that warm the oval of air above their heads, so they look like gnomes who skate-walk on crystallized water. We all giggle, even Babci.

We dress in black, but we laugh, she says, to keep up our hearts.

I think, to keep hearts from sinking in snow, in sadness. Hearts want to rise, like trees.

After the service, at the very small reception, the son from Don Mills comes over to speak to us. His name is also Dr. Kowalewski. He has a deep crease in his forehead between his eyes and a penetrating stare, as if he's wearing contact lenses that hurt. I wonder if he's going blind, too.

Babci must have told the elder Dr. Kowalewski about my art. Now I wish I'd thought of drawing him. I could have even done it without him, being blind, even knowing. But I would have asked, first. If I didn't it would be sort of like taking away his pillow.

He left instructions for me to have his art books. His son provides proof.

Edmonton, 1995

Dear Kasia,

My art books are for you. Choose those you wish. Take even those not in English, for it is the paintings that

matter. You must go to Europa to see them for yourself, and then they will be yours forever, even if (God
forbid) you go blind like me.

Dr. Konstanty Kowalewski

His books, protected from harm. For me. His arms stretched
wide like an opera singer, eyes blank in anger at his very own
son. The son supervises as I select them, at his urging, that very
day. The art books may have originally belonged to his mother,
because later I find some sketches by her, signed Jana, inside
some of the books. By the dates, they are of old Dr. Kowalewski
when he was young, when his eyes were alive. I ask the son if he
would like to keep any books for himself, and he whispers at me
to hurry up because the Goodwill truck is coming to take the
rest away with the furniture, so I don't mention the sketches.

Instead I say that his father often talked about him.

Really, he says. And it punctures his briskness for a moment.

I wonder if Dr. Kowalewski really was a bad father. I sus-
pect his son grew up without knowing him. Imagine not knowing the story of the pillow.

Inside his old pillow, we found flower seeds from his mother,
I say, and we planted them in the back by the steps.

From Poland?

We washed the pillow. You could put a different cover on it.

The son doesn't answer me, but he listens to all I say. The
feathers are from far away and long ago, from his own babcia
that he maybe never met.

As I open the first book and make my selections, he gets
his boots and goes to the back door.

I pack two boxes full of gorgeous heavy books in various
languages.

René Magritte: L'essai de l'impossible. He makes me feel like anything is possible.

Maitre de l'imaginaire: Marc Chagall. His dreams come true.

Auguste Rodin: Sculptor of Everyman. A realist, like Dr. Kowalewski.

Gustav Klimt: Das Graphische Werk. Ornate, detailed, mythic.

Op Art: Victor Vasarely. So cool and modern.

Jean Arp: Dessins, Collages, Reliefs, Sculptures, Poesie. This one, too.

Amedeo Modigliani, Angelo della Tristezza. Those elongated figures, I don't know, but I'm curious.

Aubrey Beardsley, Slave to Beauty. There are stories here.

Henri Matisse: Radical Invention. My favourite.

Leonardo da Vinci: Maestro del Rinascimento. Leafing through, I find Babci's *The Last Supper!*

Pablo Picasso: Une Vie. He knew he was a genius, but I like that he says he stands on the shoulders of the artists of the past.

Dziękuję, Dr. Kowalewski. Thank you.

His son returns from outside, cheeks pinked. He shows me his palm, covered with seeds.

They're Evening Scented Stocks. From my babcia. The seedheads were peeking out of the snow. I'll dry them and plant them in a special pot in my garden. Glad you mentioned them.

So am I.

He transfers the seeds to an envelope, folds it carefully into a square and tucks it in his breast pocket.

The abundance of the gift of books almost stops me from going back for the second box, but the son has already hauled them out on the front step for me. I hurry to get there before the Goodwill truck driver, slowing to a stop. The son props open the screen door with a box of dictionaries in many languages, and the Goodwill man takes bags and boxes and everything away. I wonder where that pillow is. Maybe it's with Dr. Kowalewski in his coffin. Oh, I hope so.

I spend the rest of the afternoon creating a thank you note, guiltily telling about the sketches I found, but two weeks later when Dad and I come by, my note is still there, and the For Sale sign is up, so I take my card out of the mailbox and burn it with one of Babci's beeswax candles. Dad makes me do it outside in the snow. I let the smoke rise up, an offering to my angels, including old Dr. Kowalewski now. Like the little white feather, the sketches of him now belong to me, but I keep them tucked in their books so only I know.

EVERGREEN

GET THOSE DIRTY CLOTHES off the floor. It's disgusting in here!

I give Mom my pity look: eyes wide open, staring her down. Seriously? I'm actually sorry for her, because if my bedroom is all she has to think about, it's pathetic. I close my door and lock it, but she has to finish.

Cassie, clean up!

As if. Cleaning up is for when you're worried or stressed or someone is coming over. That's when she cleans, anyway. Each time she comes home from the hospital, like today, she cleans. Babci's getting a pacemaker to help her heart pump. To keep up her heart.

I stay busy, too, so I don't think about it, but I don't clean. Forget that. I like my room the way it is. Piles of clothes on the floor comfort me. I can see my entire collection at once, and find anything in a sec. Colours love to be jumbled up. I don't mind a rough mix of clean and dirty; somehow it all evens out. And when something surfaces in a different place in the drift, the colour changes depending on what's next to it. I love that. Serendipity. I love that word, too, the surrender in it. I pity those like Mom who don't get it.

My aubergine T-shirt looks great with my indigo jeans.

The lemon one is perfect with the tree frog green underlayer.

My forget-me-not faded blue jeans go great with a sunset pink tank top.

I get ideas by seeing how the colours fall together on the floor. How do you get inspired to dress for high school with stuff neatly folded in a drawer or hanging in a closet? Clothes need to circulate! When they're floating amoebas they flow, find each other, generate new outfits.

Mom's the one who showed me when I was three that, to put a puzzle together, you have to see all the pieces at once.

A pacemaker is a piece that is extra. The extra piece isn't supposed to be there, but it has to fit in.

I open the window telling myself it's the oil paint that's smelly, not the floordrobe, which is so not the same as the one in the boydom of Charlie and Tom, who are slobs. Everything on their floor is beyond dirty, and when the smell starts wafting in the hall, Mom makes them wash it all. Outside, Stella swings a stick, jumping over benches and slashing the air. I yell to her.

What are you doing?

I'm defencing myself!

Stella shows me some twirling moves, landing on crouch feet, stabbing like a lunatic. Mom goes out to watch. She's actually amused. Good for her. She and Stella hang out a lot. She lets Stella get away with anything.

She's got a weapon, Mom, I call out.

She's dancing.

Defencing, says Stella.

What happened to the weapon-free zone?

Fencing is a sport.

Fencing, yells Stella.

Different rules for every kid.

She looks up at me, but doesn't reply.

The boys and I were never allowed to use sticks or stones or even finger guns. We had to go to friends' houses for water fights.

Guns are for killing, Mom always said. No violence on my watch.

Ha. Didn't she see Charlie and Tom at each other?

Playfighting, she'd say. They'll grow out of it.

Okay, so maybe they have. But it's not fair that the boys' room has been a disaster since the beginning of time and Mom never bugs them about it. Well, maybe once a year. I'm getting her grief every week, as if she has nothing else else to say to me.

Now she's cleaning up her clay pots. She usually leaves them out all winter. This year they're getting their dirt dumped out and then stacked up in neat upside-down columns in the old playhouse.

The pacemaker is even picking up Mom's pace.

I drift back to my desk, to get away from her and her hassles.

Terra cotta will look great with the evergreen I'm looking for. What's in my head is always better than what I get, but nothing captures colour like oil paint. Acrylics clean up easily but oil, oil intoxicates. Not that I know what it's like to be drunk, but I've seen the boys come home sick and strange after team parties. Charlie and Tom always make sure one is less out of it than the other, and one gets the other one in and away from Mom's eagle eye and supersonic ear which, come to think of it, have not been up to speed lately. I'm up way later than Mom. I draw at night before bed. Especially when Dad's away, I make sure the boys are home before I turn off my light.

Dad's been travelling more than usual. Mom's definitely less steady when he's away. Like he's a windbreaker for her. She doesn't yell when he's home.

The tree I'm drawing is in wind. It's fall, and there are trees losing leaves around it, but this one is a lone pine. It's about to be noticed by everyone because soon it will be the only tree still clothed, in true green. A true green that changes with the weather. That's what I want. This wanting, and finding, is that floating feeling I've felt so many times before. I keep at it, in pursuit. More yellow, a little purple, even a drop of orange. The green is working. I try it in different corners of the room, different lights, and I'm surprised how true it is, in sunlight, lamplight and closet dark. It's a beauty, and I hope I've made enough green to do a couple versions of the tree.

I ignore the calls. I can't stop even though I'm getting hungry. This tree needs more branches, and I have only a little paint left. I don't want family lunch. Dad's not home anyway. I pretend I'm still cleaning my room by knocking around some laundry baskets and letting a new array of clothes spill on the floor. I take a moment to appreciate tangerine and deep purple sweaters tangled up, which makes my true, true green on my practice canvas even more shocking.

The paint is so smooth, so luscious. Like Italian gelato. I wonder if the colours taste how they look. With the tip of my sable paintbrush, poised like I'm doing lipstick for *Elle,* I test the red, leaving a tiny clot on my front tooth. I look in the mirror, and my tongue spreads the red over the white of my teeth. The taste is sharply toxic. But I breathe it out and go for the green. Creamier in texture, the green dot goes off centre on my lip where I one day want a piercing when I get up the guts. Tastes like gasoline. My mouth fills with saliva, ready to swirl with the paint. But I can't swallow.

I run to the bathroom, trying not to gag. My mouth is a volcano, spewing puke red and green goo and alarming brown strings of spit. I swish with water, but it doesn't help. I brave boy germs and gargle straight from my brothers' bottle of questionable green Listerine.

You used to have a moustache of coloured dots from sniffing your felt pens, says Mom.

I cough in the sink. She reaches behind me for a Kleenex, holds my chin and removes a dot of green from under my nostril. She bunches up the tissue, cleans out the sink in one swipe, but catches me at the top of the stairs and guides me down to the kitchen.

Everyone else has gone to the park or Saturday afternoon practices. Mom keeps her distance, as if chat might scare me away. To her, the first law of life is nutrition, so that comes before room cleanup or I'm sorry and immediately after poison control. She flicks on her French CBC and serves me tomato soup and toast, with spinach salad on the side. She quilts quietly while I eat. She wears her glasses like Babci does, a little low on her nose.

The red soup is plain today, no basil leaves floating in it. The salad is verte, with none of the usual red and orange peppers or purple onion rings, with a clear vinaigrette that gives les épinards a slight gloss. I slurp and munch to Montreal jazz, my mind on my painting, my true green pine. Terra cotta red energy radiates from its trunk.

BLOSSOMS

WHY DON'T WE EVER have any Band-Aids?

I'm snarling on a Monday morning, super peeved. Everybody noticed my hand last week at school and I'm not going today without covering it up. Ugh. Why me, why now? I consider wearing gloves all day. I have Art first, and I can wear my white cotton gloves with the fingers cut off, because we're drawing today, so I'm safe there. Can I leave them on all day? A fashion statement? They're so sweaty and dirty, I don't think so. I hunt around the back hall for my old grey hoodie with the extra long sleeves. It will cover right down to my knuckles. If I hunch all day.

Mom says, I'll buy a box of Band-Aids when I get groceries this week.

She takes a look at my right hand, my drawing hand, and there they are: one large and six small gross warts.

When this week?

You know they go away if you forget about them.

As if.

I answer the doorbell. There's only one person who shows up at eight in the morning, our neighbour who is ninety-five years old and reminds you of that every time you see him.

Hello, my beauty! Look how you blossom before our eyes! Is your charming mother at home for a ninety-five-year-old gentleman?

He takes my right hand in his, which is leaf-dry but Superman-strong, and kisses it smack on my warty knuckles!

He whispers in my ear, I'm not flirting, I'm French!

I hide my plague hand away and watch his lips for possible wart growth, then usher him in to my Mom, who now has a surprise early morning coffee guest. They like to speak French together. Monsieur Gérard, or The Old Gent, as Mom calls him, gets up at five every morning, does his rowing exercises to "Stayin' Alive" by the Bee Gees until six, dresses and eats breakfast until seven, then writes correspondence on his typewriter with two fingers and is ready for French conversation at eight. He's like a hip Dr. Kowalewski, an unsick and unstoppable version of the pillow man.

When I ask Monsieur Gérard how he keeps up his schedule, he points to his double-knotted high-tread new white running shoes.

You know the advertisement for Nike? Just do it!

I zip up my grungy hoodie and hope no one notices my dive in the style department. Being invisible has never been my thing. But that's all I want, today.

I try not to draw attention to my right hand all week. I resist looking at it, which totally works in Art because of the drawing gloves. I need them so I don't smudge the graphite because my hands sweat on the page. I even sprinkle cornstarch inside the gloves to soak up the sweat. I thought the sweating was from excitement, but Mom thinks it's hormones and, like the warts, will go away. Her nonchalance is maddening. Her belief in the benevolence of the universe, of the future, is ridiculous. The sweating is getting worse.

You notice it more because you're drawing more in high school, she says. Every lunch hour in the art room.

The gloves she found me help, a lot. I don't wash them. I like that they're covered in ink, in charcoal, in paint. And that no one else in my class has them.

I'm okay in Gym, too, because we're long-distance running. I run by myself and gaze at the trees that ring our school ground. I take wide long breaths for beneficial, hopefully anti-sweat, hormones. The fresh cut grass smells good, too, but since I found out it's actually a distress reaction from the plant, pure anguish, I don't get off on it anymore.

At lunch, it's impossible not to look at your hands when you eat. I consider not eating, but I'm too hungry. I eat with my left hand. No problemo. Then I try writing lefty in Social. Wow. I can do it, and I get faster as the class goes on.

I've heard of ambidextrous people. Dad told me my grandpa was one. His teachers forced him to write with his right hand. It's cool to know I've got something of him in me, because I never knew him.

My right hand sits in a different 'roo jacket pocket all week, having a good old rest. I wonder if the reason for the rotten warts is because I write and draw so much in class. Some days my hand feels like it will fall off. I take constant notes to keep awake. If I don't, my mind wanders out the window to the trees and I miss out. When I'm not taking notes, I make diagrams and charts and pictures of what the teacher is saying on rough, recycled paper, which is all Mom buys. My right baby knuckle rubs nonstop.

But no more. From now on I'm using two hands. I'll alternate each class, that is, if the warts ever go away. What if I end up with warts on both hands? Then I'll get wooly black gloves with the fingers cut off like the Little Matchstick Girl. I'll drop past grunge to the dumpster look.

So be it, as Mr. Kaplan says. He's always talking in Shakespearean lingo. It's actually catching. I find myself quoting Mercutio from *Romeo and Juliet* to myself. Zounds. That dreamers often lie.

Every other day my last class is English, and today Mr. Kaplan lets us read for the whole period. So my hand is home free. Turning pages with my left is a breeze. I get a kick out of what a suck Romeo is and wonder why Juliet even goes for him. I decide that she's really repressed, and it wouldn't matter who the dude was, she'd hang off her balcony for him, as long as he's young and stupid like her.

Dad took me to see the movie. It was an actual date, my first one with a guy. How sad to have it with your own dad, but it was weirdly fun. I think Mom was even a little bit jealous. Dad thought it might help me appreciate *R & J*. He set it up between all his travelling and even bought a jumbo popcorn and a Ginger Ale for me, and black licorice in a giant package to last us the whole way through. If Auntie Magda was there, she'd be crying from the very first scene. Leonardo DiCaprio tried really hard, but I didn't cry. I actually laughed a bit into my straw. The kissing scenes are definitely awkward when you're sitting with your Dad.

Academic purposes, he whispers.

Okay, Dad.

It was a bit of a thrill, though, to be out on a weeknight with him. It felt grown up.

The warts are still there on Friday in English, when the guy to my right hands me a note, and I'm forced to take it with my afflicted hand. It's from Ricco two rows over. He's Italian, studly and dark-eyed.

Wanna go to DQ after?

I glance over casually at him and nod.

Is this, like, a real date? My hand dangles like it's been hit by lightening, and I replace it in my pocket with the note, which gets squished and rubbed with sweat. My eyes are on the page but there's a Grand Canyon in front of me for all I know. I decide what kind of Blizzard I'm going to get – but will he want to share one? No worries. The left hand will be fine with it. Straw in, hold the icy cup with the left. The mashed note in my right pocket feels like it's on fire!

The bell rings and I don't rush because I'm not sure where I'm going to meet Ricco. Then I see him waiting at the end of the hall and I hurry it up at my locker, but on the walk over to Dairy Queen, the guy has nothing to say. He's either totally shy or totally dumb. But he's not a jock like my brothers. I've seen him behind the meat counter at the Italian Centre, calmly slicing meat while I redden and run to the nut aisle. But inside DQ in the line-up he smiles at me, and I'm Juliet.

While we wait for our order, he flips open his cell phone to take a call and while we're sitting it keeps on ringing. And he keeps on answering, and talking in that monosyllabic short-hand that makes guys sound like their entire vocabulary consists of fifteen words. He doesn't erupt into Italian, which would be interesting, but he's listening to a high-pitched stream of it. Like he's late for work or something?

When I realize that I actually had more fun with the Old Gent at eight on Monday morning, I get up, my Blizzard half-full. Strawberry Cheesecake comes off my personal menu for-ever. He's on the phone again. I realize that he and I haven't exchanged enough words out loud to make a conversation. I need another way to communicate here. I take out his macerated note from my pocket and before I can stop it, my right hand draws a straight-line non-smiley face on the back of it, drops it on the table, picks up the Blizzard, chucks it in the garbage and opens the door to the afternoon.

On the way home, I take the walk instead of the bus. I shove the hoodie into my backpack and my right hand balances the straps over one shoulder in the mellow September sun. I let my cloistered hand breathe. My backpack feels featherweight with my right hand back in action.

There's a box of Band-Aids, the clear kind, on the kitchen counter. Mom makes spareribs, a mountain of them, and asks if I had a meeting after school, on a Friday. I only smile. Yeah, with the lamest Italian stallion since Romeo.

Are you going up to draw for a bit?

I nod.

You can take those to your room if you want.

She points to the Band-Aids and some mail with her knife.

I wave thanks with my right hand. I can feel the strength pouring back into it. It's ready for drawing, gloves off.

I pick up the card, from Freddy. He's weeks late, but he didn't forget my fifteenth birthday.

Auguste Rodin, *The Kiss*. Wish we could, love Freddy. How romantic. I think a long-distance Romeo is best, because you don't have to see him up close. Or talk to him, even. Or be a victim of his confused hormones, never mind your own. Last year Freddy sent Auguste Renoir, *Bouquet of Chrysanthemums*. Freddy and waiting.

I toast Freddy with some nail polish. Tomorrow is Saturday morning art class, at the art gallery. I'm wearing my tight tangerine shirt and black jeans. Even though they make you wear paint aprons over your clothes, I want my nails to match so I decide on Mandarin Mist. It's a bit brighter than my shirt, so its name doesn't really correspond with the colour but, as Babci would say, it mix good.

I love colour names on cosmetics and used to fantasize about being a colour label-writer.

Cranberry Spice is Mom's lipstick.

Roman Red is Babci's.

Auntie Magda likes Nectarine Toffee or Pagan Pink. She never wears red with her tan and blonde highlights.

I only buy the ones that make sense to me, that truly say the value of the colour, so I mainly use lip gloss because I don't actually believe most of the colours. I appreciate authentica, as the Old Gent says. But nail polish is different. It's for fun, and I like feeling the smoothness of my nails. It makes me feel put together.

I paint the left hand first, out of habit. Then I activate my newfound ambidexterity. I've never found painting the right hand difficult, but I always go slower. I challenge myself and go the same speed. And there it is, done in the same amount of time. No blobs. What a skill.

Then I look closer. The six warts are gone, like blossoms that have dropped from the branch overnight. Even with my magnifying glass, there's hardly a trace. The big one, the wicked instigator, still protrudes, but it's less ominous without its minions. I consider angel power. I've been concentrating all week on finishing a tree series on roots upturned into the air, a school project I handed in today. The side-reaching roots form a canopy of their own, unearthed and exposed. I got the idea from Mom, who hangs her geraniums upside down on a string along the garage ceiling for the winter. Then she reroots them in water in early spring. I love that those dried out roots can grow again.

I don't want to jinx it so I don't give the warts another thought and wiggle my fingers in front of the window to dry the nail polish faster, sending the fumes outside, like incense, to heaven.

TREES ENTWINED

AUNTIE MAGDA IS GETTING MARRIED.

Everyone is surprised and we can hardly wait to meet Lowell, her fiancé. She's kept him a secret, never brought him over for Sunday dinner or anything, but says they've been seeing each other for a while.

Babci is beyond delighted. She is in ecstasies. She even made chruściki, delicate sugar-dusted deep-fried loveknots. Auntie Magda will finally wear the dress lovingly created for her many years ago and, of course, it still fits. Babci will bead it now. And then, she says, she may quit sewing. Her eyes are tired, even though they still twinkle. Her eyes want a wedding.

Babci's two hands flutter over her pacemaker.

Kasia, little birdie, don't wait so long like Ciocia Magda. She presses my heart.

I don't know why Auntie Magda is getting married at all, because she likes being on her own. But then I'm introduced to Lowell.

He met Auntie Magda at his orthodontics office. She wanted a little tooth straightening and found herself a fiancé. Babci has always wanted a Polish doctor for her Magda, but with Lowell, the doctor part cancels out the need for the Polish part in her equation. For my Dad, who is neither Polish nor a doctor, Babci invented a new formula that perfectly describes him: Handsome, Handy, with Height and Holy.

Of Babci's essential four Hs for husbands, Lowell's got the Handsome part covered, but he's not Handy at all. He says he's not outdoorsy. He lives in a condo and buys everything new. Auntie Magda laughs that he replaces anything that doesn't work the same day.

She and I dropped in on him once, because they're going to live at her condo and rent out his, and she's doing the deal.

When she tells him the offer, he throws his cell phone against the wall. I pick it up for him. It's still working. When I give it back, his nails look manicured, polished. They're in better shape than mine.

Thanks, kiddo, he says.

Not anymore, I say.

She's a gorgeous young woman, Auntie Magda says. And she spins me around. Look at her gentle curves. You are going to look so elegant at the wedding! People will be watching you, not me.

Lowell, though, checks his phone all over for superficial damage.

He doesn't take the offer she found, and rents out his condo to his friend instead.

His skin is definitely moisturized. And tanned, but Auntie Magda tells me he fake bakes, at a tanning salon.

Do you? I ask.

Oh, no. It's not good for me. He says it makes his teeth look whiter, for clients.

He's tall enough, but not enough Height to change a light bulb. Not his thing, anyway.

And he's not Holy. He swore at that one. But Babci doesn't seem to care. She is swept away, as are we all, by his looks: dark curly hair, straightest of bleached smiles and a stubble beard that Auntie Magda often strokes with her fingers before he catches her hand and kisses it. I think I'm in love, too.

The wedding is going to be at the Holy Rosary Polish church, but there will be no mass. This, Babci is willing to accept. At this point, with her pearl Magda permanently thirty-nine years old, Babci keeps her mouth zipped.

But to me, she says, I whisper the mass, in Polish, and no one in the church knows, but it counts. My angels help me.

I am going to be the bridesmaid! Actually, junior bridesmaid because I'm only sixteen, but really because there is no groomsman. Lowell has a cousin but he can't make the trip, from Australia. Stella is twelve, too old to be a flower girl, but she is anyway, so it will be only us sisters walking up the aisle for our Auntie Magda.

No one wants Babci to make dresses for Stella and me, because she tires easily now and has trouble seeing, but she says these are her last dresses, for her Kasia and Sasha, which is what she still calls us, and she will do it. But I will help. We pick the simplest of designs, an empire waist for both, and she has been saving the most exquisite satin, off-white, like the bridal gown, but with no beading or veil. Thank goodness.

I have to undress to my underwear for the fitting. Babci slides the strong yet smooth palms of her hands around my bare middle. The tops of her hands are gnarly and papery.

Such a nice waist, she says. You keep it. Keep your waist.

She takes such care over my dress. I could wear it for my own wedding if, like Auntie Magda, I keep my waist. Babci adds lace to the bodice, and it makes me feel like a bride-to-be, which I am, as maid of honour. We cry a little when it is done. I tell her that I'll wear the dress at my own wedding, no matter what. She's already thought of that. She's made the side seams extra large in case I need to take it out a little, later, much later, for when I marry. If I ever do.

Make sure you marry. No be alone all your life. You make food anyway. So? Make enough for two. Why not with a man to make you feel like a queen?

I wonder how cooking for Lowell will make Auntie Magda feel like a queen, or if he'd ever throw the dish against the wall.

But Babci is thinking of Dziadziu. And feels like a queen, even after all these years he's been gone. Her jewel eyes of spruce blue sparkle when she remembers him and her head lifts as if she wears a crown. I haven't noticed that shining yet in Auntie Magda's eyes, or Lowell's. In fact, I haven't seen them look into each other's eyes yet. Lowell often inspects his hands.

Auntie Magda takes Babci and me to the cemetery to tell Dziadziu about her wedding. I wonder why Babci doesn't just talk to her Dziadziu candle but this is pretty big news, even though Lowell cancelled at the last minute to rebook patients for today so he can take the week off for the honeymoon later. Babci isn't too upset that Lowell and Dziadziu won't "meet." Mom thinks it's because Auntie Magda has been close to marrying several times, but always backed out, so again Babci says nothing. Babci wears a gold silk kerchief tied up tight even though it's a warm sunny fall day and Auntie Magda keeps the top of her convertible up. Because Mom and Stella can't come either, I am the only one from our branch of the family to go to the cemetery.

It's going to be a small, family wedding. We only have three weeks to prepare, so I am over at Babci's for a few weekends working on my dress and Stella's. Babci lets me tack down the facings and do the pressing. Auntie Magda wants the wedding before the winter, so Babci doesn't have to go out in the cold. Since her pacemaker, Babci moves slower. She constantly rests her hand on her heart, as if the pacemaker is a pet, or another hand.

The doctor said Babci should eventually forget that it's there. Nie, nie, I don't, she says.

She talks to it. She scolds. Too fast, like a toy clown, you wind me up!

Sometimes, abruptly, she has to sit down. We've brought a folding chair, so she won't kneel for her prayers by the graveside, but she does anyway, using the chair only to get down and up. My job is to take the old flowers and put them in a plastic bag. Babci likes to crumble and sprinkle the dried up Dziadziu flowers over her vegetable garden to keep away slugs. Next I have to wipe out the metal vase with some paper towel. Then I pour water from a 7-Up bottle into it while Babci adds her blessings to the already holy water.

I also get to unwrap and arrange the new flowers, brought by Auntie Magda from the florist: brilliant irises, the rich blue of the autumn sky; yellow chrysanthemums, Babci's favourite; and red gerbera daisies with straws around their stems to support their heavy heads. I add the greens last, cedar boughs. I smell them first, so fresh and woodsy. I know the green will far outlast the blue, yellow and red. The flowers look even more intense against the black gravestone, black like the coal my Dziadziu mined in the river valley. Far below the roots of any trees. Where he made rooms in the rock from the very coal he shoveled and, car by car, sent outside to the sun. When the boys and I found his miner's headlamp in the jumbled garage, an island in her garden, Babci let me keep it to remind me of him. I wish it still worked, for night sketching. Charlie and Tom found pieces of coal to keep, and even played street hockey at Babci's with a flat puck piece.

In the cemetery stands a corner of tall Norway spruce. Their branches try to reach up but droop down like curtains.

Some seem entwined, holding each other's crossing branches. They must have been planted a hundred years ago to protect their ground people from wind and noise. When I walk near enough to touch them, I feel the heat of the afternoon sun radiating from their boughs. Charlie and Tom and Stella and I used to play in them, shooed off to expend our energy away from where Babci knelt, on Easter visits to Dziadziu.

Today Babci is not sad. She has that glow, like a queen. She and Auntie Magda are speaking Polish, a prayer. I think it's the "Our Father" because I hear the word for bread, chleba, as in "Give us this day, our daily bread." I wonder if bread really means bread here, or time, "our day." I'm squirming and Auntie Magda puts her hand on my shoulder to make me still. I realize that my time, my day, is not the same as Babci's and I try to be patient for these prayers to end. So we can have tree cake, sękacz, a sponge cake with a cross-section of dark and light layers, like the growth rings on my old tree cookie. But it's *boughten,* out of a little Bon Ton Bakery box tied with string. Babci hardly has any and declines to leave some for Dziadziu as she usually does when it's her own. It's definitely not the same, much sweeter, but I happily eat the leftovers. Auntie Magda indulges in her usual one bite only and hands the rest to me.

You're just like Charlie and Tom!

No, they'd be fighting over it.

You're still growing.

So we hem your dress last thing, says Babci.

Auntie Magda lights a thick white candle with a deep well for the wick, which protects the flame from the fall breeze when we leave. She resists lighting a cigarette during the entire outing, because of Babci, who has trouble breathing. Babci blames Dziadziu's death on his heavy smoking, although I wonder about coal dust.

So Auntie Magda chews Nicorette gum when she's with Babci, snapping it. It's usually Mom who brings Babci for her Dziadziu visit because Auntie Magda is always working. She has never liked cemeteries. You can tell by the colours she wears: today she is in the hottest of pinks. But she prays to her dead father, here with her mother, that her marriage will be loving and long. At least I think that's what she's saying. I don't understand the language, but I am a witness to the words. Me, and the trees.

At the wedding, in my two-inch cream heels, I walk tall like Auntie Magda made me practice. Dad agreed to escort her up the aisle, but not give her away because, as he says, Auntie Magda is her own person, not a dame to get or give. Mom is in the front row, and supports Babci's arm when she stands up. Babci is beaming, and Mom smiles at me, too, but she still seems less thrilled than the rest of us.

But Auntie Magda is bringing us Uncle Lowell, I want to shout to Mom. Maybe it's the rush we've been in to get ready. She's had a lot to do, like getting the boys in suits. When did they get so good looking? Charlie and Tom both have Dziadziu's dark hair and day-old beard. They also each have a dolled-up blonde girlfriend on their arm. But I feel like a princess, like Babci says I am, and she gives a little clap when I pass her, holding the flowers, creamy roses. If Auntie Magda is the queen today, Babci is a queen mother! She's always admired the Queen Mother.

During the ceremony, Babci behind me speed-recites the entire Mass in Polish, like she said she would. After, I put on my creamy fleece cape that Babci made last night, in case it is cold on my arms, and it is, for October 31 (Halloween was the only available date at the church). I step awkwardly, holding up my swishy gown, into the limousine with Auntie Magda and Uncle Lowell. I want to be the first one to call him that.

They light up cigarettes like they've been waiting all day, and sip from a silver flask they've stashed in the limo. It's engraved with their initials: L and M. They offer me some, and I want to, but I suddenly feel like the kid niece and I don't want to take the chance of dripping on my dress. I tell them about Babci's private head Mass. Auntie Magda howls. Uncle Lowell drinks some more.

I ask Uncle Lowell if I get to dance with him.

If you want, he says.

Auntie Magda nudges him.

Sure, he says. You pick the dance.

I have my hair done in an up-do. It's got too much stinky hairspray, but it holds in the wind for pictures. We shiver for plenty of those, with multiple photographers, in the trees by the Legislature after the wedding. By the time we get to the reception, I'm starving.

The beautiful wedding dinner is at the Macdonald Hotel. The decorations are exquisite, all live greens and creams. We have a few speeches, even a short one from Babci, who gets teary and tongue-tied, ending up in Polish that only Auntie Magda and Mom understand, because they cry, too. Later Mom tells me what she said: Dziękuję Bogu za rodzinę, przyjaciółl i dziedzictwo, thank God for family, friends and my heritage. People have stopped listening and I get up and escort Babci back. It's bad for her heart to get upset. She kisses me after we're seated again at the head table, and some of her tears wet my cheek. I leave them there, pretending they are angel tears, because they are tears of joy.

She says to me, Kocham cię, Kasia.

I love you too, Babci.

Now, there is no one for her to worry about. Unless, now, it's me.

I wait for my chance with Uncle Lowell, but he never catches my eye because he's busy dancing with Auntie Magda. They look so good together in the golden light that everyone else only watches them. Charlie and Tom's bleached blonde girlfriends in their little boutique dresses and borrowed pearls are also in awe, but they were sure chatting each other up while Babci gave her speech. Then, even Charlie and Tom looked at each other in solidarity, but they didn't say anything to the girls.

After the speech, I'm in a washroom stall and I overhear the girlfriends.

So boring!

I was dying!

How can they stand it? All that Polish.

I come out with my best two-inch heel posture.

Because she's Babci.

The girls blink at me. But I'm not finished.

You know how Charlie and Tom say the Eagle has landed? From when the guy walks on the moon? That's what this is, for her. Talking through her speech was rude. Not cool.

They dash out of the washroom. They don't even say sorry. I hope I never see them again.

Later I nibble on wedding cake, and realize that the bride and groom have also vanished, to change. They return in their going-away outfits. They are off to Hawaii for their honeymoon, both in stylish cream cruise wear that matches the roses in the room. Everyone takes photos. The band plays for them, and Dad brings Babci back halfway through the song because she's had enough, her hand on her heart, and he takes me to the dance floor. In my heels, I'm almost his height. Dad's eyes smile and wrinkle at me. I used to stand barefoot on his shoes when we danced. This turns out to be the last dance. The band packs up, we gather up the gorgeous flowers to take home and my night as maid of honour is over.

Not long after that, there are many phone calls from Auntie Magda. Mom quilts, her head at an angle to support the phone.

Magda, calm down. Slower.

I pick up the other extension. After all, I was part of the wedding. I should know.

Auntie Magda says, I thought we were good friends, and could enjoy each other's company, and you know there are times when you need an escort, and he dresses so well ... but he only thinks of himself! He ignores me. He barely looks at me. He's out with his buddy almost every night.

The same guy, Mom says. The one sitting with the parents at the wedding?

Yes. Him. The one who rented his condo. I honestly don't know what's going on.

But Magda, you knew Lowell how long before the wedding? Two months?

I had to. You know that. For Mama.

I thought so, says Mom, so quiet it hurts.

I knew I could get out of it if I had to, but I didn't think it would be so soon. I thought after Mama...

And I see the wedding for what it was: staged, a play, a performance. Auntie Magda loves Babci so, so much that she fashioned a piece of art to show it.

Mom's needle rides through layers of fabric in silent logical lines, while Auntie Magda's wails unravel her fantasy. No one says anything to Babci.

AUTUMN COLOURS

BLACK IS THE NEW COOL. I'm done with colour. My inner rainbow folds over, and colour melds into muck. I think of it as black, but it's brown-grey-black. I'm hollowing to black from within. I smooth on the black eye shadow, which accents my darkened, thickened eyebrows.

Mom says I've got a little black rain cloud over me.

Ha. She should talk. I was flipping through old *Chatelaine* magazines for textured images to use in a collage and look what I found. I didn't know Mom wrote poems. I made a secret photocopy before I gave the original back to her. She folded it up.

Oh. That, she says. I wondered where it went.

I like the black in it, I say.

I was having a hard time that day. I went for a walk in a park near the hospital, waiting for Babci's pacemaker operation to be over. There were crows.

This time it's my turn to say it. Oh.

There's no title, so I add that.

> There Were Crows
> Crows watch the weather:
> beaks pointed all the same,
> black parasols in a tall dead tree,
> spaced,
> exposed,
> poised for an onslaught.

The calm is uncanny.
No calls from these bleak birds,
only intermittent
chatter of the lesser kind,
oblivious to portents of disaster.
Crows wait.
Until,
in utter unison,
they unfurl umbrella wings to delinquent skies,
screeching in dread delight
at the drenching, glistening release of rain.

I used to like shine, but not anymore. I'm going to black like a portentous crow. I reject facial jewellery, arm decoration, chain links, buckles, buttons and studs. I'm minimalizing. Zippers are okay, but silver only. No gold of any kind: yuck. My wardrobe has been purified to neutral: black, white or grey. White is strictly for contrast, to make the black look blacker. My skin is naturally white, and I'm hardly ever outside. I snack on ropes of black licorice, the thinner the better. I drink:

Black coffee.

Coca-cola.

Pepsi.

Dr. Pepper.

Root Beer from A & W, if I cheat.

I wear black-rimmed sunglasses when I eat dinner, to thin the glare of colour in food. The new me.

Sixteen.

Sophisticated.

Cool.

Mysterious.

Dark.

Deep.

I'm back to charcoal. I found a box of charcoal sticks and pencils from when I was seven, when I made that robin sketch that Mom moved upstairs to her new master bathroom.

I blame that red. The red of that robin. I started using colour too early. I need to go back to black. Start over. Feel line, crusade for contour.

Picasso.

Miro.

Rodin.

I've added to my charcoal box, more thicknesses in browns and greys and new blacks, and I'm working on texture and shade-fades. I'm back to essentials. I'm at home with bare tree branches. I've put the pastels away (was I once so seduced?) and the paints I used to taste (so juvenile, like Stella, who eats dog biscuits when she's feeling ratty) and the hundreds of collected European pencil crayons (my first intense love) for later, much later, or maybe never. Right now it's all about line.

Graphite pencils are for when I'm on the go.

On a napkin at Tim Horton's (over a lonely cup of cheap black coffee).

My arm (temporary tattoos).

My notes (de rigueur for arties).

A faded brick wall, waiting for the bus (removable graffiti).

Charcoal dust marks my fingers, roots in my hand lines, scuffs into black jeans (no more cotton drawing gloves).

You must be an artist.

It's this guy at the bus stop. I'm drawing a dog. I reply after a pointed pause.

I like to draw.

I wish I could do that.

Which is what they all say. Passion envy. I recognize this guy, Brian, a jock.

Why, I say.

Why not?

It's a curse.

Because you like to do it?

Because you have to.

Or what?

Or you feel scummy.

Scummy?

Yeah. Like you suck.

So, it's like an addiction.

Yeah.

What else do you do?

I don't answer. Usually people are scared off when I don't answer. Actually, the dog I'm drawing is barking at him. But this guy must like dogs. He keeps asking.

You wanna walk?

Over the bridge?

Yeah. To the next bus stop.

Why?

I dunno. Autumn colours?

I guess it's okay to look at them. I don't have to ...incorporate them. Brian reads the newspaper, or the headlines, anyway. At least I think that's ink on his fingers. Sports section.

I put on my black-rimmed sunglasses from Auntie Magda, the foundation for my recent new look, and we walk. Brian is pretty chatty; I am purposefully restrained. I listen, sort of, and stop to gaze from time to time, posing: my neutral against the canvas of nature. I feel pretty cool in the breeze on the bridge. I don't let him have my sketchbook, but Brian, two heads taller than me, carries my math book, which I've personalized in black pleather. His hand is sweating all over it. I'm going to have to wipe it off on the grass. Brian talks about school, the news, basketball.

So do you want to go?

Okay.

Before I realize, I've agreed to an hour in a stinky gym, with yelling people and shrieking whistles and high-top shoes screech-stopping at the pitch of screams. Streaking red-yellow-blue-green uniforms and hairy armpits. And bouncing, the incessant bouncing of a large orange ball: my brothers' innate weapon against my personal serenity. I haven't played basketball since Annie left. I can pin it by that gap. And since Charlie and Tom went away to university, the basketball net at home has been abandoned. Brian has snagged me in a moment of nostalgia.

I'll take you for pizza after.

I'll probably just have coffee.

See you tonight. He grins.

He wipes off my book on his sweats and in a whirl of leaves, amber-wine-aubergine, he gets on his bus. By the time my bus arrives, I feel confined in my black tights, knit skirt and layers of grey-black-white tops. My feet complain that, to walk in comfort, my black Mary Janes can't compete with Brian's size thirteen Nikes. I give in to the streaming flow of tree colour, traffic blur and bus motion. For once the colours don't blend to brown muck, but flick light and strands of green-yellow-blue and I wonder why, mesmerized.

In a haze I block out dinner scramble, dog panting, soup spill, sister whine, parent callouts on times and places for pick-ups, and escape upstairs.

White bedspread.

Buffed hardwood.

Clean surfaces, tools neat.

Papers stacked, books in colour order.

Grey-white-black clothes hung up with space between. Colours in baskets below, discarded.

Sanctuary.

Changing into my faded black jeans, I consider dying my hair black. It's already espresso dark brown, but black would be better. This weekend.

Brian pulls up in an electric blue midsize after everyone has gone out. Louis is there at the door to meet him. Brian gets both hands full of dog slobber. The dog and Brian are in fits of mutual adoration as I hug my sketchbook over my coat.

Cool, he says.

Maybe he means Louis. I think he means the sketchbook. Maybe he thinks I'm going to draw him. I am. I need to reduce his world to black and white.

But I don't draw at the game. I'm magnetized. I can't take my eyes off him, because he's usually the one with his hand covering half the ball. With the ball he's a god with long muscular arms. His legs are springs, hopping from spot to spot. He's so nimble, hyperaware of where all the other players are. He doesn't hog the ball, but his teammates usually pass it back to him and he scores over and over again. And if he fumbles, he doesn't fume about it like my brothers do; Brian calmly recovers it on the rebound. His confidence emboldens me. I cheer for him, by name, at each play; I'm sitting on my sketchbook now. I want to dance with him, have his hand flat on my back. He doesn't look at me once; he's totally focused on that ball and that basket. And so am I, right up to the standing screaming 45 to 39 finale.

Waiting for him to shower and change, I'm one in a tight cluster of girlfriends, younger siblings and parents expelled from the steamy gym. Behind the locker room door, I hear water streaming, guys hollering and laughing, locker doors slamming.

I'm waiting for a true athlete to take me for pizza. But I feel like a waitress. I've got my sketchbook under my arm like a menu. Should I dump it in the garbage can? Run it up to my locker? Split? What was I thinking? A Grade Twelve guy? A jock like Charlie and Tom? Who eats whole pizzas folded and stacked like quadruple-decker sandwiches?

But he's so hot. And I want to be cool.

I escape from the clutch of people discussing details of the game (is that what I'm supposed to do?) but Brian catches up to me like I'm not running away and steers me to his car.

We're meeting everyone at Boston Pizza, he says.

I want to go home, I say.

Are you sure?

He sounds kind of hopeful. Like maybe no one else is home yet. He looks at me sideways. I change my mind. This is a group date. Everyone. I wonder who they are.

Okay. Let's go to Boston.

Okay.

And he's not fussed about it. He's easy. Like he intercepted a fumble and scored. So I tell him.

You were amazing. That was a great game.

He grins. Did you get a sketch?

Sorry.

Too fast for you?

Yeah. Maybe.

At Boston, the pizzas are already on the table. Did he preorder? Or is this a regular deal? The other guys don't take notice of me, but the girls do. They have French manicures, hour-long hairstyles, recently shaved and tanned legs and clothes fresh out of an expensive shopping bag. To them, I'm an art rat.

The blonde busty one says, Cassie, right?

Hey. What are you having?

The guys eat, says Tiffany, chewing her gum.

We never eat. That's Morgan.

We have tea. Herbal. The bleached alpha boobs, Jennafor, as in forward.

I'll have coffee, Irish.

As if I'm eighteen and legal. Which I'm not. But Brian is, and orders it right away.

The pizza smells and looks delicious. Brian offers me a bite from his piece and I take one, closing my eyes for effect. When I open them the girls' mouths make identical os. I select a whole piece for myself.

I count up the jewellery points on the triplets. I used to be attracted to bijoux and glitter, but trees are naturally without it. I'm going to have trouble at Christmas time, because even the thought of tinsel on a tree makes me ill. But Brian's shimmering arms and shoulders transfixed me during the game, so I tell Brian that the silky blue and gold basketball uniforms are eye-catching.

Anything to catch yours.

That shuts up the girls. They watch me request extra ground black pepper on my own slice of three-meat pizza with black olives.

I flirt with the guys some more, and tell them I'd like to draw them in motion at practice. I want to see those muscles move again. Brian's, specifically. They thumbs-up the idea, and talk about framing sketches for their moms for Christmas. The girlfriends' eyes swell and stare at each other.

After my Irish coffee, I look up at Brian like we've known each other forever, and we get up, wordlessly, in sync.

He helps me put my coat on, and his hand on my back as we walk out feels great. I can also feel Tiffany, Morgan and Jennafor eyebeam me as we leave.

I don't think Brian usually brings a date to after-the-game pizza. I think he's trying to get the attention of Morgan. Of the three, I hope it's her. Her smile to me seemed real. She senses what Brian is up to. I'm out of my league, and she knows it.

In the car, Brian says, I'll check with Coach, and I guess I'll see you at practice.

Monday after school?

You're sure, he says, like he's not.

I need some more figure drawings for my portfolio. I'll be there.

While I gather up my sketchbook, he jumps out of the car and runs to my door to open it. As he shuts the door behind me, he kisses me once on the neck, and then walks me up to the house. On the steps, my sketchbook jabs him in the ribs and inside, Louis starts his I-want-some-too-barking, which is what he does when anyone is hugging someone else. Brian kisses me once more, this time on the forehead, teasing me. He opens my front door and keeps kissing me as we move inside. I let Louis hold my sketchbook in his mouth, to shut him up, and kiss Brian with Irish coffee lips and two hands. Colours start whirling in my head. The colours intensify.

No one home? Brian murmurs.

Guess not, I mumble.

Mmm, he says, with a long and lean kiss, and I'm feeling his shoulders now. They feel like they look.

And his hands are up my shirt, unhitching my bra. I catch Louis' look, perplexed, and he gives a little growl that permeates my Irish coffee brain.

Sorry, you have to go, I say. They'll be home any second.

Is that why?

I don't even know you, Brian.

He pulls back, gives me a look like that play didn't go the way it should have, but he's got another one in mind, and maybe he's going to go back and check out Morgan.

In three elastic strides, Brian's in his car and burning out of sight, and I know he won't be back, and I won't get my basketball practice sketches, but the colours in my head continue, circling in a kaleidoscope. Shades I don't remember. A new palette from an unknown planet. A planet of boys.

Dave.

Jerry.

Tim.

Rufus.

Dennis.

Hues and intensity and shades blend with boys from before:

Freddy.

Darryl.

Ricco.

I turn off the light and crouch in the dark, my hand circling the dog's back, trying to memorize brightness, tonality. To ground this brilliant world, get it down on paper or canvas or an old white shirt. One of the colours is basketball orange, sweaty and warm from Brian's open hand, and in motion. All of the colours are in motion.

LATE SPRING FROST

WE'RE IN JASON'S WHITE Toyota pickup, making the first tracks down the alley in feathery May snow, rounding like a dream into the driveway. Jason cuts the lights and the motor and pulls me to him again. We've been out watching the stars by the river. The dinky clock shines 4:09. The only sound, our breathing. The lane light sparkles snowflakes. Inside, kisses, skin on skin, warm again.

There's nowhere else I want to be. We've been going out since we met at a New Year's party. Kimmy, from junior high, introduced us. But before that, his grey eyes picked me out across the basement rec room, kept looking over at me, so I looked back. Jason and Kimmy go to a different high school. He had just broken up with his girlfriend and bleached his hair blonde to celebrate. He's in the last year of the automotive program and works for his dad at a garage. He likes that I'm from a different school. His old girlfriend was clingy.

But we're pretty into each other now. Out every weekend. The party tonight was at his friend's. We stayed the latest, as usual. Then went to the ravine. His dad doesn't care when he gets home, as long as he's at work on time and takes care of the truck until he pays it off. I'll be tired tomorrow, but I usually make it for Saturday morning art class at the gallery. Not sure they can teach me anything anyway, but I'm way behind on my final portfolio for school.

We don't hear the van until it cranks up the driveway beside us, doors slamming in the middle of the night. Dad opens my door, yanks me out of the truck and calls in to Jason.

What the hell are you doing bringing my daughter home at this hour?

Mom hits Jason's window with the palm of her hand. Jason flips his baseball cap backwards and fast-turns the pickup down the driveway, skidding on new snow, and my car door slams shut by itself.

Snowflakes waft down on my nose and hair, trying to keep me in place, but I run after Jason, slipping on snow tracks. Dad, breathing hard, catches me from behind, arms tight around my waist. He lifts me up, twisting me back toward the driveway.

I hate you, I yell.

I'm a siren in a white wilderness. I kick at the air and plow Mom in the hand. Dad pushes me in the gate and I break away, running for the lock on my bedroom door.

Mom keeps her voice low.

We were at the hospital. Babci had a stroke!

I hear Stella crying.

Stella whispers, I tried to call, but you wouldn't answer your phone!

Mom takes Stella back to her room and doesn't return. Dad's steps are heavy on the stairs. He passes by my door without stopping. Doors close down the hall.

Quiet as dust, I collapse to the floor. My dead cell phone slides out of my bag, under my bed. I let it be.

I will myself not to stir. A stroke. That means paralysis. I make my limbs stay where they land. I ache for Jason.

For Babci. I wonder if it hurts to have a stroke.

Cramped, every muscle stabs. My thoughts, twisted ropes; my heart, pounded flat; my guts, shrink wrapped. My ears ring. My eyes sting. I make no move.

The stillness of the house, when I get up off the floor, startles me. Is it that early that everyone's asleep?

I wonder if I'm alone. In an alarming new way, I am.

I get up, bone by bone, so stiff I can hardly stand, pins and needles in every muscle. My purple sketchbook is halfway hanging off my desk, about to fall, so I take it, my arms acting out of habit, scooping a pencil, an eraser into my jacket pocket. My brain is whitenoise, grey screen. All of me feels heavy and prickly.

Downstairs I snatch a can of juice from the pantry. Cranberry, my usual first choice, but it burns road rash down my throat, ragged from screaming. I sip it slowly to make it hurt more. Outside, my gripless flats gather in snow, smudge the thin calm white way to the hospital. Nothing appears in my path. At this early hour, no traffic interferes with my silent trajectory.

It's way after hours, so I stand in the cold light of the hospital door a long time. Finally, a group of worried relatives in saris and slippers come out; they hold the door kindly for me, but I can hardly mutter a word of thanks when I go in. My throat feels stopped up.

Babci's room is dim. She sleeps.

I open the curtains, but nothing in the sky breaks through the dark. No dawn light. No moon. Not even a scribble of cloud.

I crouch on the windowsill and sketch, leaving out the tubes and the breathing mask. I work on the meshed lines of her face, deeper than I remember, caressing each one with my pencil. I draw her eyes the way I want them: open and shining and bright. The feeble break of day reveals delicate leaf-vein creases on her chin. Her breaths have no pattern, and more than once I freeze my pencil, waiting for the next inhale. My stomach gurgles.

A nurse checks in. Her cheeriness exposes me: a hunched troll.

Have we had a good night? Good girl! Lucky to have a visitor so early!

I pause, in awe of this nurse, name-tagged Patsi, a chirping bird among the old and sick.

May I take a peek?

I show her the portrait so far.

Your grandma is beautiful!

The lines around Patsi's eyes dredge with real concern, care. A kind of love.

I wish someone would do this for all of them, she says. There's so much beauty here that no one sees.

Patsi puts both hands on my shoulders for a moment, and the two hills there melt into a prairie across my back. My mouth involuntarily nudges open. My throat a raw fist, I can only nod. She waits for it, my manufactured smile, and takes it with her to cock-a-doodle a patient behind the curtain to yet another day.

When I finish the sketch, Babci sighs. It takes a long time for her next breath, and I don't breathe until she does.

In this dry close air, I'm sputtering and choking when Mom comes in. She pats my back and hands me a tissue. My sketchbook slips to the floor. She picks it up, studying the portrait while I wipe away snot, spit and tears. I force my voice until the growls morph into words.

Mom, I don't hate you.

Finally, she says, I know.

She looks at me from a new distance, face to face. We're on opposite cliffs now, but we'll never take our eyes off each other.

I wonder if Mom ever kicked and screamed at Babci. Then she adjusts the oxygen mask on Babci's shrunken face, smoothing out the torqued elastic across her ear and I know that, in her own way, she has.

My hand shakes as I start to rip out the page, the last one in my book, and pass it over. Mom's hand stops me.

No, you keep it, she says. For your portfolio.

The purple bruises on the back of Mom's hand from when my foot kicked her last night curdle my guts. I run to find a washroom and then a payphone to call Jason. I get his voicemail.

Yeah, call back, I'm out.

I do. Sorry about last night. I'm at the hospital with my grandma, but I'm going home now. Phone me when you get this message?

When I get home, Dad grounds me. I've never been grounded before.

No Jason until after finals.

What?

And your portfolio is handed in.

Dad!

He's distracted you from it, Cassie. And from yourself.

How do you know?

He's made you... anxious. You're happiest when you're at your drafting table.

Dad's hardly looking at me. He doesn't come in my room, but stays in the doorway. He knows I'm not a little girl anymore. So why does he want to pin me to my art table? He doesn't even like my art.

What about a curfew? What if I got in at midnight?

We already tried that, Cassie. No. It's only two weeks. He closes my door.

Before Dad takes away my cellphone, his old one that he pays for, I call Jason again. I get his voicemail again. I rush my message, not sure how to say it.

I'm not allowed to see you till after exams! My last one is the 27th of June and it's over at 4. I'm going to go crazy not seeing you. I'm sorry. I really, really am.

Jason doesn't call the house phone, but then he never did.

To pass the time, I sleep a lot.

Stuck in my room, I have no interest in studying for exams, but I settle back into my evergreen cone series. They're realistic, so they take time, focus, attention to every fascinating detail. I've been collecting for a while, and I wanted to have a mosaic of diverse cones, a community: pine, spruce, fir, balsam, cedar, hemlock, larch. After many false starts, I finally loosen my markings, move away from the actual, and the cones get a little more impressionistic. They go faster once I relax and let go of perfection. The first ones look messy, but gradually I get a rhythm and they soothe me. I keep working, and eventually the floating feeling comes back, I'm out of my head, until I think about Jason, and then I wobble and dive back into bed.

Lying there, I think about adding insects—ants, beetles, a worm—when Auntie Magda comes up to my room. I haven't seen much of her since Christmas, when she and Lowell were still married. They waited until the New Year to get their divorce. I've been wanting to ask ever since.

Was that planned?

No, no, my darling, no. Not really. I mean, I didn't know if it would last. The men I meet, they don't stay. I get tired of them.

Jason said the same exact words to me, about his girl-friends. It makes me shiver. Auntie Magda sits on my bed, and hugs me to her. She digs in her bag.

I brought chocolate. From a client, but for you.

Take me away. I want out of this house. Mom treats me like an alien and Dad's being a homework cop. I can't do anything.

No. Here's why. You have a family here, I live alone. I put on that wedding, you're right, for Mama. It was for her, but I hoped, I really hoped, it would be true. But Lowell and his friend, the one who took his condo? They're a couple. He's with him. And I'm alone again.

I stop unwrapping the bar of Swiss chocolate.

So why did Lowell go through with the wedding?

Same. For his parents.

You both did that for your parents?

It's stupid, now we know. We liked making the wedding, but we couldn't make a marriage. It was expensive, but in one way, it's good we tried, because now Lowell knows for sure. He's a much happier man. We still have lunch.

I thought I could believe in you.

Her hand reaches in her bag again. Oh, no. Out comes her Kleenex. She's going to cry.

Auntie Magda, no.

I wanted to have my own job, make my own money, have my own car. Mama wanted me to marry. I did what I wanted. And now I know that it's absolutely right for me. Not that I won't stop looking for a wonderful man, but I love my life as I am. You do what you want, but don't leave your Mom. Not like this. Not now.

She sniffs and wipes her eyes, expertly salvaging her mascara.

Now, taste your chocolate and get back to your work.

And I do. The chocolate helps.

After Biology, my last exam, waiting in his pickup is Jason with that loose smile and those steely eyes and I'm rescued.

Hey, Babe.

Drive, drive anywhere, go any place, get me away.

Yeah?

He's looking at me, touching my hair, waiting to turn left. He leans over to kiss me, and we creep out of our lane, and get hit by an oncoming truck. The sound of crunching metal reverberates in my ears.

Jason holds on to his left shoulder with that arm, catches blood dripping down his ear. I'm calling him, Jason, Jason, but he won't answer. With his other fist, the one nearest to me, he bashes the steering wheel. He keeps punching it, again and again.

My neck is ratcheted; my head screams pain. My seatbelt was on, so my head didn't hit like his. I don't think I'm bleeding, but there's windshield glass in my lap. The pickup clock face is cracked.

I want to call Mom, but I don't have a phone.

There's a siren coming at me, piercing my skull. Someone opens my door. Then they carry me away.

WHITE WOODS

THEY'RE SENDING ME TO art camp for the whole summer in Deadsville, Alberta. I'm packed up, prisoner in my neck brace in the back seat. Dad drives the Chevy van a shade over the speed limit down Highway 2. Mom keeps her eyes on the road.

Dad is saying this town's not so bad. The boys had lots of tournaments here. They've got a decent rink, and there's a burger bar near the soccer centre. On Main Street, Mom gets excited about a quilting store. Oh, and there's a 7-Eleven. Big whoop. I know why they're doing this. Because of Jason. They're abandoning me for six weeks.

The whiplash hurts, the neck brace is a bitch, getting dumped in this dive sucks, but not hearing from Jason is the worst. Not seeing him, holding him, having him hold me, making every cell of my body alive and awake.

The camp building, a community college, sprawls low, a grey slab. Prairie burnt dirt and weeds lead up to a black door, scratched and abused by boots. But inside the door are bursts of colour, walls covered in student art. It invades my swollen eyes with light, hue, exposed prairie perspective. I can't look away because of the neck brace. So I cover my eyes and ears as my parents lead me to my room. A barren single room without windows or room for three bodies to linger. A bed, that's all. And a closet. Then they kiss me, the shell of me, and leave me there. On the way out, they promise to call. I don't. I phone Jason instead. I leave messages.

Hey? Call me?

Like, maybe you could leave me a message?

Are you there?

All I feel now is flatness, funneling to a pit. The beige of my dorm room spreads out around me. I slide into a hole of emptiness. I can't imagine seeing anything, much less making anything, here. I'm in a desert.

I spend all my time after morning drawing classes in the studio. I skip painting. I don't want colour, even watercolour. The instructors don't care, as long as I'm working. I keep my pencil in my right hand so I can't hold my phone, another hand-me-down from Dad, but with a new phone number. Administration has already confiscated three phones from the careless.

They've supplied me with a fresh sketchbook, poster-sized, with a black cover, which I appreciate because I'm back to black. But this time, that's all there is. I don't even see colour, could care less about it. The black book conforms to my black jeans, black T-shirts, black zip-ups and a black City of Champions baseball cap, a parting gift from Charlie and Tom, home for the summer just as I'm gone. I wear my hat backwards.

Stella, bewildered by the accident and my abrupt departure, found me a fresh white eraser from the kitchen school supply cupboard. By instinct, Stella knew I needed something to squeeze as I angled my propped throbbing neck into the van. I fisted the soft eraser the whole way here. I keep it in my left hand, in class and out of class, and compress its warm blanched skin. I search with my pencil for something, anything, in the blank howling sky of the page.

I can't move my head in the neck brace. I can't look down at my work, so I feel even more distanced from my hand. I can't bend over it, cobra down and up and move with the page. I'm trunked in this brace, like a tree myself.

Louis barks and whines, so I let him out of the yard when Dad made me rake the grass as a fresh air break from studying. I scraped the ground to wake it up, get green, get alive, after this winter that stretched into May and a truncated spring that forgot to rain. Louis plodded over to the bunch of trees and bush on our lot we call the wild area. It's left over from when our house was first built, part of the ravine. It forms a screen from the front street and contains windsong in the aspens, the promise of Saskatoon berries, the natural rot scent of its mini-forest floor. By the time I bagged up the piles of dirty dry grass, Louis chose the shade of a chokecherry tree, flopped down facing the house and died. He made sure that I found him, not Stella. We buried him in the ravine.

The next day it rained. The green came into the grass, but Louis was gone.

The grass here is a variation of beige. The wind dries it out and no one waters it. My stunted windswept trees attract the attention of my teachers.

Intriguing, they say, one by one. Hmm.

They're looking for a tendril of growth, a drop of moisture, a bit of grit. A pulse.

The students are a mix of city and country kids, here to have fun.

Hey everyone, we're playing Twister in the lounge tonight!

I turn my body and braced neck the other way, obviously excluded but pretending not to hear. They have even less interest in me than I have in them. After drawing and painting and sculpting all day, they want pizza parties, reruns of "Candid Camera" and loony board games.

All I do at night is check my phone. All I want is Hey, Babe.

I don't care where the tears fall. I smudge them away. Or not. I let them buckle the paper for texture. Mom and Dad call every day. They go on about the boys' basketball and track coaching gigs and Stella's volunteer job at the animal shelter, but I only listen to the bits about Babci, still in the hospital. Weak. Sleeping a lot. Not eating. They don't say so, but I figure it out. Babci and I, both captive, displaced, lost. I imagine her eyes. Her eyes are open, faded lights in a tunnel. I focus on that flat blue, searching for a flicker. I say nothing. I hang up when they talk about me. They're also on the phone with Administration. Everyone expresses concern about me. Everyone except Jason.

Two whole weeks have gone by and Jason has still not phoned. I know he's out of the hospital because they said he left the next day. More and more, I don't know what I would say to Jason if he did call. Not: how are you, since he doesn't seem to care how I am. Not: do you miss me, because it's pretty obvious he doesn't. And not: I'm sorry, because what am I apologizing for? For him not calling? For him putting me in a neck brace? For getting me sent away? For ghosting me? For losing the will to draw? For being so lonely I can't even dream?

I chuck my baseball cap to the back of my closet.

I think of Babci, she and I, both stuck. Will she ever be free of her hospital bed? Will I ever float again? Do I want to?

I picture us out of the tunnel, facing a drape of fabric, the blankness of the page, the white of invisible woods. We hold hands. We wear fleece capes. We walk on top of the snow. It sparkles.

The trees, encased in snow, are snow ghosts. Like on our family ski trip to Kelowna, the trees reveal no evergreen at all. Instead, they are crystallized with sticky, windblown layers of snow that imprison them. All that is left of the tree is its rudimentary shape; it is a ghost of what it once was.

Yet my snow ghosts on paper look like creatures, people cloaked and hovering, animals hollowing inward. Frozen in the act of being.

Babci, bending to pick up a pin.

Louis, keeled over.

Stella, on all fours, nose to the ground, teaching her new puppy.

Me, reaching to the sky but missing, arching over.

My instructor tacks them to the hallway gallery in a line at eye level on deep green cardstock.

The third week in the camp cafeteria, watching my food get cold and letting a thin trail of tears slide into my soup, someone stops at my table. A guy in a black T-shirt brings me soft ice cream from the industrial stainless dispenser, loopy and filigreed into one of my snow ghosts, slightly leaning over the edge of the pink melamine bowl. He rubs a spoon on a paper napkin to shine it up and pokes it in the base of the ice cream tree, supporting it now so it stands straight. I don't look at up his face, but I notice a red stubbly beard. He fills out his T-shirt like a farmer. There's white writing on his shirt: Eat me. Then he's gone, and from the back I see he's solid, stocky, and walks like he's at home in this place.

I feel like Alice in Deadland, but I eat the ice cream as instructed. It melts a crust on my scabby heart. Now there's an open wound.

The next day, I need a balm. I serve my own ice cream in a discreet simple twist. The black T-shirt guy builds a dramatic triple-decker in diminishing proportions and eats it, across from me, without a word. Except for his shirt: Michelangelo rox. He's older than the other students. For two more nights, he and I meet at the ice cream machine, addicts, and sit down in collusion, black T-shirts oblivious, silent, pure.

The fifth day, ice cream boy wears a red shirt with a stick-on retro nametag lettered in red Sharpie: Hi, my name is Matt.

I wonder why I never see him in class. Maybe he works in the kitchen. He doesn't talk to anybody else. His next T-shirt is back to black, with a fresh photo transfer of the white marble *David*. So that's his deal. I should have known by his ice cream creations. I didn't sign up for sculpture.

Check out the studio?

I can't nod my head with my neck brace, but I pick up my sketchbook and follow him to Sculpting. He turns on a battered CD player. It's Bach. Strings. There's clarity in it. It stimulates me, finds feeling in my arms, shoulders, neck, where it was numb.

I slide down the wall, sink to the floor and draw the sculptures in progress around me, simplifying three dimensions to two. The white plasters become organic shapes on my page, like clouds or dandelion puffs, airborne. I feel the contour of the sculptures with my pencil, as if there's no distance between the plaster model and me. My hand is on the shape, yet the pencil is on the paper. I'm floating again. I'm so grateful.

The next day, Matt clears off a drafting table, tilts it almost vertical for my arm and eye and finds me a chair. He supports my back with his hoodie folded up into a cushion. Then he sands his plaster. He sands, then feels with his hand, smoothing, touching, feeling the bite of the sandpaper into plaster. It's white, like our vanilla ice cream without the shine. He's sculpting a head. It takes me a while to recognize that it's mine.

We don't talk much, but I follow Matt to the sculpting studio each night after supper. Sometimes, random shudders shake out of me. My shoulders ease a little. And then more. After a week, I shove the neck brace in the corner of my closet. I'm breathing deeper, like Matt, who gets a full-body workout every night chiselling and scraping and sanding. That's after he works the early morning stocking grocery shelves, and sculpting class all day. No wonder he eats so much.

We adjust the drafting table for standing height. It feels good to stand after sitting in class and in studio all day. It feels good to get closer to the paper, put more pressure into my markings.

I check out the Bach CDs on my way out one night, and the next day Matt gives me a freshly burned personalized one to keep.

I draw Matt sculpting. I make him a little more ripped than he really is. I ignore the little beer belly, but I keep the thick neck, hair long to protect against the prairie sun. I emphasize his powerful forearms, his broad hands. I make his beard a little trimmer. Then I write in some hidden messages in my pencil markings. Cool, in his shirt pocket. Hot, in his jeans. I title it, too: *Matt-er*. He makes me sign it and decides it's ideal for a T-shirt photo transfer. I make a cardstock frame, the colour of his eyes, a little darker than Babci's, wishing he could find a T-shirt in that spruce blue. He puts my sketch up in the window by his workstation, which seems to be his and only his. Later I find out he's the administrator's nephew. His parents want him to take over the family grain farm.

I probably will.

What about art school?

Can't afford it.

What about scholarships?

I'm a self-taught kind of guy. Besides, I have to be here seeding and harvest. There's no one else to do it. I'm planted here. But I can make the rock move.

I think of Freddy in Europe, the art cards he's sent me, and silently vow to send sculpture photos, exhibition catalogues, books, anything to keep Matt sculpting out on a farm.

Winters are long here, Matt says. Lots of time for sculpture. And I need to eat.

In the late July heat wave, I eat salads, but they're as wilted as I am. Matt confines himself to the fried food selections. We try to outdo each other at the ice cream machine. His grow taller, architectural and turreted. Mine remain bonsai.

I put on the weight I lost, I say.

Your jeans fit better.

It's all this ice cream.

Matt licks his spoon. I want to do you nude.

I laugh. It's the first time I've opened my mouth wide all summer. I laugh loud and long, and everyone in the cafeteria is entertained, giggling. I'm suddenly hilarious. I catch my tears on the back of my hand and whisper to Matt.

Why not?

We lock the studio and make sure the windows are completely covered.

If you jump me, I'll stick you with a sharp pencil.

He pretends he doesn't hear as I come out of the corner workstation with my sketchbook open lengthwise, its spine hugged in line with my waist, shielding all but my limbs. I didn't think to bring my bathrobe.

I have to ask. Have you ever done a nude before?

Sure.

When?

Last summer. There was a girl. Like you. But she was chunky.

Matt!

Static. She was static.

My feet are bare and the studio floor is gritty. I slide one leg against the back of the other, feeling the softness where I've shaved. I've creamed my skin, too.

So how long does it take?

About three weeks.

Three weeks! How am I going to get *my* portfolio done?

I want you drawing.

Where do I sit?

You stand at the drawing table. I want you from the right side to start. Put your sketchbook down.

I forgot my pencil.

Here's one.

That's not mine.

Your pencil is part of your hand.

My pencil is in my bag and I'm not bending over to get it.

I'll get it.

Get the eraser, too. It's white.

Get comfortable. I don't want a pose.

Can't you start with the clothed body and do the head?

Already did the head.

Can I put my jeans on? Can you do the top half first?

I need to work with the whole form.

I need a drink.

Water. He goes out to the hall. I could run right now, but the tiny muscles of my feet push against the floor to feel my full height. Clunk. The vending machine drops the prize, and my legs settle into my drawing posture, but my sketchbook is still in front of me. Matt comes back in the door, locks it again and twists open the bottle, cold, slippery with condensation.

Anything else?

You can't touch.

I stay behind the line, he says. Putting his back to me, he comes near and uses his foot to draw a semicircle in the plaster dust on the black floor a leg length away from me.

Does that work for you?

I can't work if you talk to me.

I can't either.

I want the cello prelude in D.

I was thinking of something slower.

I want the volume up. Way up.

What about the fan?

No.

It's sweltering.

Not when you're wearing a sketchbook.

Just put it down and draw, he says.

I take my time. If we're doing this, it's when I'm ready and only then, like Auntie Magda said. This is not like being eleven, being stopped by Mr. Buddy, the creepy elementary school janitor who tried to make every girl stand straighter against the wall to display her developing breasts. This is Matt, already an artist, committed to the plaster block in front of him just as I am to my big, blank page.

Matt turns the music down. He's talking, quiet, and slow.

You're a deer in the woods, he says. Eating leaves. They're new green, still unfurling. They're irresistible. You don't see me.

But you're going to shoot me.

I'm only a photographer. It's early morning, misty. I've been waiting. I'm doing a photo essay on deer.

For who?

Bach.

Why?

Because ...deer are full of grace. I bet he was looking at deer when he wrote this. You can hear them. Grazing, but alert. Soft eyes, but solid bodies, springing the world into motion, into grace, with every gesture, every move. He turns the music up again.

And I put down my book and draw. I don't look at him. I make him repeat the deer talk every night, and every night I draw the woods the deer knows. My deer is not lost in the woods. She remembers each tree, rock, grass clearing, stream.

The heat gets worse with the windows sealed tight, and I let him turn on the fan. I feel every floating particle of air, every hair on my arm, every drop of sweat on the back of my neck, under the loose braid of hair, the only part of my costume. I'm excited by my own nakedness, by being shaped into an unknown form by Matt. As he sands his plaster, his hands are nowhere near me, but the air is smoothing, caressing the length of me. My nipples bud in the breezy warmth.

Like the deer, I'm alert to Matt's eyes, but I don't meet them. I'm not interested in him, unless I need to defend myself, but I enjoy the fluid sensations inside and outside me, my stomach digesting, my own wetness, sweat beads trickling down to my waist. On my neck, a fly perches and I blow it away without moving my head. It lands back on my arm and I let it follow the path to my inside wrist. I let myself feel everything, as if I'm the only one in the woods. I keep my pencil moving, and my markings become freer yet sure. I breathe to the music.

My trees become taller, fuller, less raggedy. They have delicate, individual leaves. The leaves grow in proportion and number, to feed my deer. An expanding canopy of branches and foliage fills the paper. Each shape reveals another.

I don't look at the rough plaster column, either. I stay with my trees while Matt makes dust with his tools and his steady strokes. When the music stops, the sound of his hand sanding, sanding, sanding blends with the motion of the fan. At the end of each session, he coughs and wipes and drapes the sculpture with a damp drop sheet.

It's about a quarter of my size, but its mass is startling.

One night, after pulling on my bathrobe, I ask, does it have a title?

No answer. I always feel ripped off when pieces don't have a title.

Or, I say, is this *Nude Two?*

Nude Two.

On my birthday, Mom and Dad call. We talk longer than usual. It's been a long summer for all of us. They ask what I want for my birthday present.

Would it be okay to move down to the basement room?

Are you sure? The light's not as good down there, says Mom.

We can amp it up, says Dad. It will give you more space to spread out your work.

We all want to get back to some kind of normal. But I want more privacy, distance. Solitude. I've gotten used to it here. Even my nightly sessions with Matt are on another, uninhabited plane.

A week later, after I'm dressed, Matt pops a mini-champagne that his boss, who's in AA, slipped to him in the caddy cart at a weekend golf tournament. The boss also won a bird carving by Matt, which he kept for his wife.

Matt pulls away the dropsheet and we drink, from clear plastic cups, to *Nude Two*. She doesn't look a lot like me, or anybody. Yet her form is female. Her hip, a shoulder, a breast and one arm. I make out the braid, but she's faceless, all smooth muscle, fired and working, culminating in the tip of the pencil in her single hand.

How was *Nude One* like me?

She was sad.

Did she get happier?

That was Bach.

You're going to be great, Matt.

Bach is great.

So are you.

I hug him, my head nuzzled to his heart. He's surprised, but he moves his hand up my back, under my shirt. I let him feel my arms, my neck, and beneath my unbraided hair. To measure. To remember. To compare to *Nude Three*.

Then I take his hands in mine. He wants to kiss me. He's murmuring his way down my face.

Don't you want to? I've been waiting for this.

But that's not why I held him and imprinted my belly with his cowboy belt buckle. I need to tell him, because I'll never see him again. I step back.

You melted away my frozen layers so I could find what I need. I'll never forget.

Neither will I.

You will. When you find *Nude Three*. And she's going to be right for you.

I let go of his hands, and we sip our bubbly like it's 7-Up. I hold my glass up to him.

To you.

To deer.

To her.

To you.

I get his address, slide it in my back jeans pocket and then kiss him on the cheek, goodbye, Matt. Then I kiss *Nude Two*, on top of her intent little head. I recognize the tilt of it.

She's alive, I say.

But I'm thinking of Babci.

Matt watches me gather. I move like a deer in the rainy woods, softly yet sure-footed.

My water.

My sketchbook.

My robe.

My pencils.

My eraser.

My key.

I go to my room to pack. The show is tomorrow. Charlie and Tom are coming with Mom and Dad and Stella and Auntie Magda and then I'm going home.

HEARTWOOD

I'M DRAWING HER HANDS.

Hands sewing invisible stitches to hem a dress.

Steadily cutting fabric with heavy shears rocking on the dining room table. Kneading delicate stretchy dough for pyrogi.

Quick sketches. Lots of restarting. I'm searching for a pose that can say what I feel. And, I need figure drawings for my portfolio. I've got lots of trees: apple boughs, the dancer tree, the grandmother spruce, the lemon tree, the exposed roots, the cemetery sentinels, the snow ghosts. But I also need portraits of people. I wish I had the basketball dudes. I've got Stella and her bugs, an easy subject because she sits still easily, and that one of Babci's face, but now I want a series of her hands.

Patting my hands together and singing my love to her: Toshie-toshie tosh-ie, mója droga Babci.

Arranging flowers in a vase, propping them up against each other, yellows and reds and purples.

Scolding, with her crooked pointer finger, but jabbing like it's a joke on me.

With the rosary, crystal cut beads draped over one hand, praying. Her way of floating, being alone and away.

Patting down a fresh tablecloth.

Planting a potato, fisting it down in the dirt.

Brushing crumbs off the table and spilling them from her palm into the bird feeder.

Hands sleeping, like now, curved into nests, on top of the waffle hospital blanket.

Attached to the IV, taped and bruised.

I try to find the exact position that will keep her hands alive. I wonder if I'm working in the right medium. Maybe the hands should be clay. But Matt said stick to what you know.

Make your drawings sculptural, but don't make sculpture unless you're willing to start over.

Okay, Matt.

So I keep drawing. I'm going to take photos of her hands to send to Matt. He's an assistant instructor now. And he's getting married to a country girl who can do the farm books and loves the life. Will he see Babci's arms like I do? Like branches, giving me the air I need. I keep looking at them, remembering them. Searching the camera in my head.

Miss ya, Matt.

Miss you, my darling, says the letter, translated by Mom. Must see you. The letter, to Babci from Iwona, in ornate, tall handwriting.

Iwona, a friend from the mother country. She must see Babci, and stops in Edmonton for a few hours, en route from Vancouver to visit her son in Toronto. All the way from Argentina. I wonder why? Mom says Iwona referred to an urgent moral emergency. Is Iwona one of the postcard people, from the box I kept? The handwriting looks antique, old worldly. The stamp, Republica Argentina, with a map. The pictorial stamps on the back of foreign postcards intrigued me more than the distant landscapes or faded religious figures on the front. I examine Iwona's words, calligraphic, precise and measured, in a language I recognize but don't understand.

Iwona took the boat to Argentina and Babci took the one to Canada. At seventeen, the age I am now.

When they bought their one-way tickets across the ocean, in different directions, did they know it would be forever?

Did they want it to be?

Was it life and death?

Had they not parted friends?

Could they hardly wait to leave, like me?

Like Darryl?

I hadn't seen him for three years, while he was at Vimy Ridge Academy for cadet training, but this year he was a guest performer at the Remembrance Day service at my school. He's taller, broader, now more confident than nerdy. The kilt definitely works with the full uniform. And the sound of his bagpipes. Arresting. I waited for him after, while the crowd jammed the exits. His deep voice, luscious, radiophonic and commanding, surprised me.

Hey, Cassie, I hoped I'd see you here.

Darryl, hi. How's the army?

I start training right after graduation. I've actually finished my diploma already, but I'm taking a full load of foreign language courses to fill in the year. They've asked me to do a dual role: piping and intelligence work.

Wow, I say. But Darryl's already been spying on people all through school, perfecting his powers of observation by being so on the outside.

They think I have the aptitude for it. I'm excited. But if it doesn't work out, I'll always have the bagpipes. You?

Art school next year, if I get in.

Of course you'll get in. You, like me, have been preparing your whole life.

But I'm not sure I can do it.

That's the fun of it, Darryl says. We never know.

And with that, we're bonded.

This spring he sent me a letter, which surprised me even more.

Garrison Petawawa, Quebec, 1998

Dear Cassie,

We're supposed to write a letter to someone who matters to us, because we're going on a tour abroad. I can't say where, but it's a stabilization operation. I picked you because I don't really know any girls, but I feel like we have some connective tissue, at least about trees, from the day we skipped class to witness the slaughter. I'll send you some photos of the trees where I go. Do you have email?

I forgot to tell you: I checked, and I was right about dendochronology. You count the xylem, which brings the nutrients from the roots to the leaves. So the tree is "standing up," when you count, which is how they should be left, in your opinion. So I "planted" a tree in the rainforest, in honour of your grandmother spruce, may she rest in peace. Oh, and the reason the centre of your tree cookie is darker in colour is because that is the heartwood. The colour difference is a chemical reaction to make the heartwood resistant to decay. Heartwood, then, is like the memory of the tree.

Your contention that trees are like people has made me think about the characteristics that, in fact, trees and people share. They root. They transplant. They need light. They make their own food! They need rain (pain for people?) for growth. They scar. They like to live in groups. They're tough but they bend with the wind. They are wise. However, I think trees may be smarter because they don't have wars. They compete, but they coexist.

I've developed "Tree Day" into one of my more popular anthems, and each time I play it, I think of you. Our time together was the best I had at school, actually. You listened to me. Thanks for the inspiration.

Keep drawing.

Affectionately, Your friend, Darryl

He left a forwarding address so I need to send him a reply, but I haven't figured out yet what to say. That was his best time? I'll send him a care package with Squirrel Crunchy peanut butter to remind him of home and a drawing of that pissed-off squirrel, like Darryl, singing for the dead. I hope Darryl is not in danger and I wonder if he's bagpiping or spying.

Truck bombs.

Land mines.

Friendly fire.

Post Traumatic Stress Disorder.

I'll send him the feather from Dr. Kowalewski's pillow because it has already survived a whole war. Darryl needs it more than I do. The softness of it. Especially if he's really a spy. For his heart pocket.

Affectionately? How to let him know that this does not mean I have romantic feelings for him? I hope he meets someone someday. I start a drawing in my mind, a sketch inspired by Bernini's *Apollo and Daphne*, the branching hands of

Daphne as she transforms into a laurel tree. Because she wants nothing to do with Apollo.

But if I'm the only girl Darryl's reached out to, I need to be careful, especially considering where he is. And to thank him for the rainforest tree. And his trees-as-people comments. I'll draw him the squirrel. I wonder how many notes a squirrel can sing? That can be the title: *How Many Notes?*

How many years have Babci and Iwona been parted? Babci's hands show her years. They were unlined when she was a girl with Iwona.

Her hands.

Brushing her hair, dark auburn once, redder than mine.

Applying Roman Red lipstick in the mirror.

Buttoning up her navy coat, smoothing it over her hips.

Firm around my waist, pulling the yellow measuring tape.

Waving goodbye until she is a wiggling dot under her bountiful apple blossoms.

I wonder what it's like for a Pole to learn Spanish. Or anyone to learn Inuktituk.

Yeva, the lunch lady who read T-shirts, sent a note to me, care of my junior high school. The secretary mailed it to me.

> Dear Kasia,
>
> The further north I go, the more honest people are. People are here from everywhere and that makes me feel at home. My son needs me to babysit his baby soon to be born because he and his wife both have two jobs each. I will teach the baby all my languages.
>
> Your friend, Yeva

I am in awe of her, and Darryl and Babci and Iwona. If they could leave home, can I?

Iwona's silver bracelets chime her into the hush of the hospital room, followed by Mom, shaking her head like she does when she's miffed. Iwona is an elegant, erect, made-up woman. Not a dressmaker, say her diamonds, dangly earrings and wrist bling, her tan and her dyed black hair. She comes to me first and holds the side of my head with her hand.

Little birdie. That's what your babcia says.

She says the word the proper Polish way; she doesn't know my name for Babci, formed when I was so young. And she has no idea what little birdie means. When I was little, I thought I could fly up to treetops like a bird. Just by drawing. The only person I ever told that to was Babci. She called me my little birdie after that. Iwona has no right.

Bonita, Iwona says. Beautiful, that is for me. She says it with a jealous wonder and defiance as if to say: you are lucky to be young but it won't last; see how I must push away aging and the moment I give up I will die, like your babcia.

I won't look at her face; I only look at her charm bracelet, boasting memories of high life on her well-defined wrist reaching out of fur cuffs on a magenta sweater. Then she turns to Babci.

O mój Zofja, she says. Spójrz na mnie.

Babci opens her eyes wider than I've seen in a long time. She does not speak; she hasn't in months. But she looks right at this Iwona. And there's life in her eyes. I'm grateful to Iwona, right now, for lighting up Babci's eyes.

Babci reaches for Iwona's multi-ringed hand with her own wrinkled nude one, but misses, her pinky finger leaning on Iwona's thumb, like two birds side by side on a telephone wire.

Iwona puts both hands on Babci's, now hiding it under her emerald rings and magenta nails.

I cannot stay terribly long, she says.

Her English, remarkably good, is for Mom and me.

In Polish to Babci, accompanied by the melody of her silver charms, she begins with a blessing and a kiss. Mom understands, and I look to her for a translation. She's annoyed. She has to drive the boys to the airport later today for their summer training camp, but she's just come from the airport with Iwona and must get her back for her connecting flight. She's got the driving-all-day look, which flattens her into two dimensions.

She wants to be forgiven, Mom whispers.

I wonder why?

I don't know. But I bet it's about money.

Mom seems more than annoyed now. What could Iwona have to say to Babci now, for so long, from so far away?

Babci's gripping Iwona in that blue spruce stare of astonishment at the human failing of her loved ones. I've had lots of those, when I fight with my brothers, ignore my sister, tell off my parents, keep my distance from everyone. Desperate to go away to art school.

What you need more school for? You draw, like I sew.

That was before Babci stopped sewing, before she lay down in a hospital bed, before I could answer.

But now I know: I need to find other people like me, like Matt. And because he can't go, I have to.

Lasha, one of my teachers at art camp, says there is no artist who doesn't need a teacher. I need teachers like her to tell me: don't stop. Lasha gave me a card, her own design, black-eyed susans, after the final show, with three lines of script and no signature:

> Sloth is the enemy.
> Lack of belief in yourself is another.
> False priorities a third.

She didn't single me out for attention at art camp, or talk to me, but then I hardly spoke to anyone but Matt. Lasha came by my work table at least once a day, though, and uttered a soft umm, as if not to scare or interrupt me, but to let me know she appreciated my effort. She probably gave everyone the same message. But for me, it confirms my plans.

Dad says, You're set on this?

There's nothing else I can do.

That he understands. After Art, my other grades flatline.

How will you live?

I'll probably have to teach. The instructors at art camp are all practicing artists, but they teach on the side.

Then you need this degree.

Dad looks away. Sending me to art camp was his idea, but if he ever knew about *Nude Two*.... Art camp may have saved me then, but he's losing me now and he can't picture my future. Neither can I, but I know art school must be my next step. I'm sure of the step, but not sure where it will take me. It's risky, but Dad understands that. His business, oil and gas, is built on risk assessment. I like to think my taking a risk comes a little bit from him. But a lot from Babci. A country, an ocean and then a whole continent.

Iwona's clutching Babci's hand tight and they're in another place and time.

Iwona wants to be forgiven for what? For not staying together? For jingling across continents while Babci lies silent?

Is the Argentinean air so much better to preserve your skin like that? The climate? The food?

After a Polish train like a zipper carried them from the bottom of the country north to the seaport of Gdansk, if they clasped hands and ran up the gang plank to the same boat, could I have been a dancing Argentinean girl with natural black hair and sun-kissed wrists circled in tinkling silver?

I wonder what kind of trees grow in Argentina.

What kind of birds.

Iwona's got a slim flat box that could hold a handkerchief or a fine leather wallet, and she's thrusting it at Babci, who does not want to let go of Iwona's other hand. She wants to be young a little longer.

Mom has been listening to Iwona's confession.

The photo, Mom is saying, the two girls at the seaport.

I know the one, tacked on the wall above Babci's sewing machine. Young sailors with white scarves, smoking, queues to different ships, steam whistles blasting, her new white dress dyed with a delicate purple flower pattern and in a low-waisted, full-skirt style she's invented herself, with matching fabric on her smart straw hat, ribbons in the wind. This is before parting and promising to send postcards all their lives.

Iwona has brought it all back, but she opens the box, and it's going now, going, going, gone with the money, Polish zloty, funny money, spilling on the blanket, ancient purple-red-orange bills and thin tinny coins.

Mom is furious. She gets up to leave, to pull this woman away.

Babci's memory scatters. Her eyes go waxy, lidded, exhausted.

Click. Iwona snaps her purse shut, sighs and puts out her hand to me. I want to shake Iwona, protect Babci from the cut of that sound. Click, it echoes in my brain. But Iwona is muscular as well as fine-boned and anticipates me with steely strength. She limits the shake to one sure stroke, then pivots and struts out, a one-woman band of miniature cymbals. The room smells of her perfume, flowers I don't know.

She included interest and accounted for inflation, Mom says.

Mom kisses Babci, waits for my nod that I'll stay and reluctantly follows Iwona's parade. Mom's seething.

The sewing machine money, she says as she goes.

We are quiet again, Babci and I.

I collect the fallen money and return it to the box, which Babci pushes away, spilling it again. I am also offended by the clink of the coins, yet I count them up, with the bills. I need to know: 4,075 zloty.

But this is much, much more than Babci had saved to buy a sewing machine in Canada forty-five years ago. Five hundred zloty went missing from her pillowcase two nights before she left, at a farewell party at home given for her and Iwona. Babci always thought her mother took it, considering the family now had one less wage earner. The lost zloty were wrongfully blamed on her own mother all that time. And why Babci had to work at a factory for years before buying a sewing machine of her own so she could stay with her two young daughters and work from home.

The photograph of Zofja, before she became a mother or my Babci, and her tall friend, pinned above the only sewing machine Babci ever owned, rests in my box of postcards, along with drawings of Babci I made as a child, rescued by me when Mom cleaned out Babci's house this year and sold it. Mom kept the sewing machine for me.

So that was Iwona. Now I recognize the posture, that chesty stance, her store-bought suit, despite the fact that Zofja made all her friends' and family's clothes. The money. So now Babci knows why Iwona wore a new suit of pale pink wool to travel across the world.

I scoop my hands under Babci's, my palms lifting her featherweight fists. I want her to remember the hope, the promise, the excitement of that day at the ships. My hands need to know, too.

I'm glad you didn't get on the boat to Argentina, I whisper.

Babci opens her eyes to me so I say my vow out loud.

I'll never dye my hair black again!

She claps her hands, flying slowly, happily, in the heavy air, once. Like a bird's wings, they close and then open to me.

And Babci gives me the image I want for my suite of sketches. Hands like birds, here and there, doing this and that. Landing on my chin, on my head, in my dreams, with purpose, wit and compassion. Picking up threads, feathers, seeds.

Babci's hands fall to mine. They land like seed cones at the bottom of my heart, and take root.

TREE OF POSSIBILITIES

THE WATER'S HOT, BUT I don't adjust it. I take it as it comes. Being up all night chills me right through, but in the shower I thaw, relax and focus on the last of my packing. A few things left in the dryer, check the front hall for scarves and gloves, under the bed for whatever lurks there. Take it all. Pack it all up. Stuff it in. Who knows when I'll come back?

But I have to come back. For Babci.

Where are you going? When will I ever see you again?

She doesn't have to say it. I see it in her eyes. Her fear, and it scares me.

Babci, I'll see you at Christmas. I'll make you some Babci bread. We'll sing Stolat. Stolat, stolat, niech zyje zyje nam. May you live a hundred years.

I know, she nods, rubbing the beads of her rosary. Even though she's not talking anymore, she's still praying.

She prays for me, she once told me. She prays for everyone she knows and everyone she doesn't know.

Even the man in the moon?

Even him, she laughed. And Ciocia Magda.

I'm there when Babci notices that Auntie Magda isn't wearing her diamond ring. Babci rubs her thumb over Auntie Magda's bare ring finger.

Mama, buzi, buzi. It wasn't right. A little mistake. We couldn't make each other happy. But we still love each other very much as friends.

I know what Babci thinks because I've heard her say it before, about Mrs. Sekula's youngest daughter. Why leave a healthy living husband?

But Auntie Magda has hope. It's a Polish kind of hope, closely related to guilt.

I'll find someone else. You'll see.

And to me, she says, If I don't, I still have you, Cassie. You'll come see me when I'm old.

I can't quite imagine her old, because she hasn't aged at all in the time I've known her. She takes very good care of herself, but she still cries a lot. She's crying now.

We all pray for Auntie Magda in our own way. I think of her when I light a candle. Auntie Magda buys a new one for each of her lovers, and sometimes lights a lavender one for Lowell.

I think Babci understands. She kisses her own thumb and wipes away Auntie Magda's tears with it. Then grasps both of our hands as if to say, I don't want to leave you, but you have each other.

Drying off, I start to shake. Not because I'm cold, but because I'm terrified. I'm leaving everyone I love.

No one else is up yet. I shiver until my clothes are on. Enough of that. A year of planning, two scholarships and a bunch of Dad's airline points are sending me to Vancouver, the most happening place in Canada. Where it's warm even though it's wet and everyone, including the art school dudes, are fit.

According to Mom, going to art school has been my destiny ever since I picked up a crayon. All of that stuff she gave me I've packed: art pencils and metallic markers and scissors that have never let me down or walked away.

Cassie, look what I found in the dining room cabinet.

Oh! My old blankie!

I wonder why it was there?

You probably hid it on me.

Maybe I was going to wash it, or mend it. Look how torn the blue edging is.

I used to cuddle it like this.

This white fabric with the little blue flowers, Mom says. So faded now.

It felt like her hand on my cheek.

Whose hand?

Babci's.

Why?

Well, she made it.

I can see how you thought—

Babci could make anything! With her materials. And her angels. Like magic.

I know, but she didn't—

It reminded me of her. That's why I loved it.

It was before I learned how to quilt.

It looks so small now. I wonder why she made it so small?

It was supposed to be for your doll.

But I wasn't into dolls, not until Barbie. And that was only because of the clothes.

Well, I didn't know that when you were a baby.

What do you mean?

Cassie, I made it. I'll fix it.

I can see it's important to her to mend it, a task she meant to do long ago, so I give in, but not sure my kiddie blankie gives the image I want at art school.

Auntie Magda thinks I should get a nose ring. Very exotic, she said.

Mom glared at her.

I used to think I'd need a piercing to complete the look: obsessed, chic, pale. Except I can't stay inside all day for anything. I need my trees. And Vancouver? I can't think how anyone gets anything done there. Will my eyes ever get used to the mountains, trees and sea? I've promised to eat well so I won't get sick and so I can do my best.

That's the code around here. The Word of Mom.

My eyes prickle. I wonder if we'll talk on the phone much. The boys hardly ever call, away on sports scholarships in separate, but adjoining, provinces. Having the Saskatchewan-Manitoba border in between must be weird for them. Mom phones each of them, every week. Will she phone me, too? She's got Babci to worry about, going to the hospital and back every day, and driving Stella to her part time job at the pet store.

Mom comes in as I'm packing the blankie in my suitcase. We laugh. It feels so good to laugh together again. But it's my next-to-last day at home.

I found this little basket of fabrics, Mom says. Remember these?

This is from Babci, I say.

You used to feel the fur coats of her ladies. You had to touch them.

I loved going to the Polish church with her so I could kneel and feel the lambswool and the shearling or the suede of the person in the pew in front of me.

Babci cut same-sized squares of various fabrics for me to keep for myself. Later she taught me their names. She knew the English words from the fabric store signs.

Silk. Babci made me a pink silk dressy jacket to go over a strapless dress.

Velvet from a Barbie gown. I stroke down its weft, and back up to change the hue of emerald green.

Brushed cotton. The same as for Dr. Kowalewski's pillow. I rest my head on it, in my hand.

Seersucker. Stella and I had matching sundresses in this yellow print, and Mom used it in her Sunbonnet Sue quilt.

Polyester. A red boxy skirt suit that made me sweat. When one of my teachers said I looked like a red nun, I murmured, My Babci, my grandmother, is Polish.

Ultrasuede. You could wash it, and I had a dress in this navy. It also did not breathe.

Wool. Like the ouchy couch.

Tweed. Mom's suit, browns and oranges.

Satin. Auntie Magda's wedding dress, off white.

Denim from the boys' old jeans.

Flannel for nightgowns. Stella and I got one every Christmas. Charlie and Tom got pyjama pants in the same Christmasy print, always white and red. Also Polish, Babci would remind us.

Rabbit fur to make collars on special suit jackets. This was my favourite. Still is.

Leather. I loved the black smell of it. I want a black leather jacket and dropped a big hint for Christmas.

This time I say it. Thanks, Mom.

I'm taking them all with me. I may add a few pieces, and I'm going to stitch them together, with Babci's sewing machine, when I get to my dorm room. My own artful quilt of textures, or maybe I'll use it in a mixed media or sculpture project. I'm nervous about three-dimensional work, but texture is my security blanket.

I hope Babci can hang on till Christmas for me. I need her to. I suddenly want a recording of that Christmas carol,

"Lulajze Jezuniu," to sing along to her but I only know the English words: Sleep little Jesus, my little pearl, while Mama comforts you, tender, caressing. I'll find a Polish recording, the perfect present for her.

Dad's concerned that art school may not lead to an actual job. He's not enthused. It's hard for him to understand that being an artist is a way of life, and being an artist means always learning and growing and that you need to travel to find teachers and opportunities. But he's shown me how to make a budget and stick to it. And he got me a receptionist position at his office for the summer, to make some money of my own before I go.

I asked around, he said, because your scholarship may not be enough. I talked to some colleagues and a financial planner. And they said if your daughter wants to be an artist, you should put aside money to match her income, to make it equitable with every other worker.

What?

Yeah, so that's what I'm going to do. It's only money.

But it can make you crazy.

That's why I'm doing this. So you won't worry.

I shouldn't need a lot.

You won't get a lot. But it should be enough.

I'm shocked by the weight of this unexpected insurance, yet not surprised that he's actually researched and considered my future. And bonus, he gave me a duplicate of his credit card for emergencies. But the best is that he'll come to visit on business trips to Vancouver, a couple of times a year. That will be awesome, just him and me, going out to a restaurant, walking the shore. I'll get to show him around the school, my neighbourhood, the trees I make friends with in Stanley Park.

Mom thinks I should check in on Mrs. Sekula, Babci's old friend, in a care centre in Vancouver. Even though we can't communicate, I might. I would like to make her smile. I'd like to draw her smile. I've packed my lemon tree flipbook to take to her, and a photo of Babci and her apple tree.

I stash a card for my eighteenth birthday from Freddy in the flipbook that he inspired. I missed sending his last year, but mine to him this year was early to make up for it. This feels like the final card from Freddy: Claude Monet, *Bouquet of Sunflowers*.

> Thank you for all your drawings, Cassie. They are framed on my dorm wall. When I go for my thinking walks, I look at trees because of you. Let's keep in touch on email: skyreacher@unige.ch. Best wishes for art school. I'll be in Paris next term, at the Sorbonne. One day I'll be able to say, but of course, I have her originals. If you ever get to Europe, viens chez moi; I'm your man. Fred.

I'm saving to go to Paris. Maybe I'll get a part-time job. Mom thinks, maybe in second semester, once I know my way around and have my schedule under control. I want to meet the Fred who once was Freddy. Some day.

Mom wants to go to Paris, too. She even suggested we do the trip together. I wonder.

I know Mom can't come see me, at least not until... I can't think about that. It's might happen while I'm gone and it's going to put me in pieces, but I have the hand studies and that's what I'll do... when Babci goes to her angels.

I may be working on them forever, like prayers, Polish protection.

Mom thinks I should come back for a quick visit at Thanksgiving.

I should. I will.

I know I'll miss Stella. She's getting old enough to be interesting. She's going to have to do high school all on her own. I wonder how she'll do around guys. Anyone she dates will have to be an animal lover, too, so she'll probably be fine. She wants to be a vet.

I wrap up a framed piece of calligraphy Mom made.

> I am Cassie Aleksandra
> sister of Stella Mariana,
> daughters of Diamonda (Dida) Stephania,
> sister of Magda Evanjelika,
> daughters of Zofja Wiktorja,
> sister of Rosella Bacia,
> daughters of a woman in Poland
> whose name I don't know.

I really want to know the name of the woman in Poland, and her mother and all the mothers before her. There are edges I need to explore.

I'm zipping it up, latching it tight, my past, my suitcase, my childhood. Wait. I've got to get some pix of all this. I pull out my camera, my grad present, suddenly really useful.

I use a flash on the family portrait, the one before the boys left. I look so young and unaware that I get the urge to draw a self-portrait of me before myself. And my sister, hanging on to Mom, she's a big baby-child, fearless and angel-faced. I want to do a portrait of her, too. Her before herself.

One of the house, from the front, from the back.

A photo of the empty boys' bedroom, tidied and ready for their next visit. Their quilts. They're both going to law school now, so their college sports careers are over. I was hoping they'd visit Vancouver sometime, for tournaments, and I'd go to their games. But we'll have Christmas holidays at home.

I take a picture of the goofy newspaper guy, who always says hi to me, the first one up, he thinks, but really the last one to bed or not at all.

I snap a few of my old tree pals down the block, then stuff my pocket with crabapples, a little softer than I like them, for an airplane snack. I breathe in the early morning smell of the pine, and pull a bit of bark off my beautiful birch, taking care not to make it bleed. I walk the neighbourhood, in dawning light, a tourist in my own time.

Back home, I check the fridge and there's a lunch all made in a paper bag, ready to go. The last lunch. I pop it in my carry-on, and throw in a box of my personal tea for when I get to my dorm room: a narrow nun bed and a laminate desk, a tall window and a small closet. Mom and I checked it out on an overnight interview trip to Vancouver at Spring Break. I am eager to strip down to basics.

Fire.

Water.

Air.

Earth.

Fire: the feature wall by the bed. I've seen that orange before, in Auntie Magda's orange paisley bikini. Mom and I bought bedding to match, and she's made me a Stained Glass quilt of appliqué tree trunks against the sunrise, to set me on fire. Auntie Magda suggests tacking up drawings on the wall.

Neutralize the orange, she says. Never too much, or it will overtake.

I'm taking some candles to remind me of Auntie Magda despite Dad, who's disappointed that I've inherited her candle habit. Scented ones to remind me of home: Sage, Cinnamon and Pine. And a new one of my own: Patchouli. When Dad found out, instead of an all-out lecture he suggested a pickle jar of water on my windowsill in case of fire, but I'll get a cute watering can and a few plants. The window ledge is deep enough. It will remind me of Dr. Kowalewski's gulag garden. I need some leaves. I need green. I need to grow.

Go with the flow, like water.

Take it as it comes, like air.

Let it happen, like earth.

Fuel the fire within.

I'll make my windowsill the inspiration shelf. I'll collect seedpods, pine cones, wood, any interesting texture or colour or shape. And pile them between my plants: tulip, orchid, geranium. I want to go beachcombing for bits of sea glass. Some shells. I'll go for artist walks, where I photograph and breathe in and look and look closer. In the humid air. I want to devote myself to details. This is my chance.

My hair will go curly, and I'll hardly ever have to brush it. It will look better with hats than straight hair. Most people there dye black, but I like that my curls show a variation of browns. I think I'll wear hats. And keep a yellow apple on my desk to ground me.

Mom's up and managing.

Did you get your lunch? Passport, ticket, money? What about the stuff in the dryer? I'll get your sister out the door and then we'll go.

Stella comes down the stairs slowly. The basement has been my domain for the year after art camp, with way more space to work on my portfolio. To be alone. No one comes near it except to do laundry next door. Stella took over my room, and Dad moved his study back up to hers. She knocks on my bedroom door, softly. She's got a card for me, to open on the plane. And for my ears, when the plane takes off, like Dad likes to have when he flies, a package of gum, my favourite kind, cinnamon.

Have a whole piece, she says, not half. We giggle about Dad's half-piece habit, but chewing a whole piece of gum feels like too much. We've been trained.

I show her my closet, still stuffed with clothes. I've only taken the blacks and greys. The rest are in colour order.

ROYGBIV, she smiles.

Red.

Orange.

Yellow.

Green.

Blue.

Indigo.

Violet.

Grade Two rainbows, she says. I was first in my class to know it because you taught me.

So you know where they go when you borrow.

It's the first time I've seen all the colours hanging up.

Me, too.

We hug and I tell her to keep in touch. Dad's giving her his old desktop so she can email. High school sucks without a good friend, and Stella's a bit like me, a loner. A dreamer. But she's also a lover of all creatures, so she'll do okay. But I won't be here to watch her be okay. I don't think she'll call me, but I'll call her. I commit to it there and then, hugging her shy young body, but the same size as me.

I tell her that Dad wants to surprise her, and told me not to say but, sisters' secret, he's planning to bring her to see me in Vancouver once things are settled at home. Before Thanksgiving. She squealed!

We'll go to the Vancouver Aquarium, which she will love, and go beachcombing and she can take photos with her new camera that is my old one that I'm leaving for her. It actually put me in pain not to tell her before. Stella gets so excited, like I used to, wanting to go everywhere with Babci. And their trip depends on Babci, if she's stable. I figure that if the trip doesn't happen, Stella at least gets to enjoy the idea now, but if it's cancelled and she never knew, she would get nothing.

Stella helps me carry the suitcases upstairs and into the car, and then she's off to walk a neighbour's dog, leaving Mom and Dad and me. We don't talk a lot on the way to the airport, but when we get to the security line, it all spills out.

We're so proud of you.

I'll miss you!

We love you.

Love you, too.

We'll see you soon.

Christmas for sure. Maybe Thanksgiving.

I'll book it for you, says Dad.

Call us, says Mom.

As soon as I get there.

Learn all you can. Enjoy every minute.

I'll try.

Take really good care of yourself. The best.

We don't cry. We are steady. Our eyes are clear. We mean everything we say.

After I collect my carry-on at security, turn back for a final wave and walk to the gate, I grasp a sensation from when I was very young. I'm cradled by my mother in the dark, in an unfamiliar place. Strange lights startle me. We are at the edge of the world, but my mother is fixed, a rock. I know she won't fall over that edge because she holds me.

Next I see a willow ptarmigan, on a taiga trail, pure white and unafraid. My baby hand goes out to touch it, but there are only feathers, white, piled in a heap.

Feathers from the pillow of a Mama for her old man son.

Chirping in the bushes.

Sunlight pouring in my head.

Nests across the world.

A pearl.

Angel smoke strands from a candle.

The gaze of a deer.

Floating and drawing, drawing and floating.

My little birdie.

An anthem to honour the end.

Babci in my heart, in my blood, in my heartwood. Babci, the inhale and exhale of her name. The first thing I'll do is send her a postcard, mail from me, when I land in Vancouver airport.

Settled in my seat on the plane, the man with thick white hair next to me puts away his newspaper.

Good morning. Is this your first flight?

My first flight alone, I say, and wonder how he can tell. He has a vintage Canadian flag pin on his red corduroy jacket.

Ah, a magic carpet to another place.

I hope not too bumpy.

Ah, if there are bumps, it means there are clouds. We are interlopers in the clouds, so we must permit them to jostle us from time to time.

I love ...the clouds. I like your jacket. The colour.

So my friend will find me at the airport. This red is ponceau. From the red poppy.

Ponceau. I have a new word already.

Are you going to Vancouver to study?

Yes. I'm going to be ...I'm an artist.

Ah, you are a lucky one. Me, at your age, I wished to be in your place. But we had a war. And after, I had a barber shop.

I think of Darryl and imagine him as old as this veteran and I have a spurt of serenity. I'm suddenly certain that my bagpipe spyboy will be safe. In the same instant I feel the urge to draw the whole world. The old man puts away his glasses in a green alligator skin case.

But did you keep drawing? I ask.

After? Ah, only in my head. And now, with my arthritis, it is not possible.

His hands, like mitts, fingers locked in a stiff curve, holding what stories, what treasures, what roots.

Would you mind if I draw you?

Maybe later, when we are in the sky. Then I will be the ideal model ...still, except for my snoring.

As long as there are no bumps!

Ah! That won't wake me. There will always be bumps, my friend. Like the glorious trees in your path. He's seen the trees in my sketchbook on my way to a blank page.

We fall quiet. His body settles, heavy, craving rest. I wait for the man's eyelids to flutter and close.

My pencil on paper climbs the ancient branches on this man's face as the airplane rises above the cloud bed.

I am away.